Also by Crystal Thrasher

The Dark Didn't Catch Me

Between Dark and Daylight

Julie's Summer

(MARGARET K. MC ELDERRY BOOKS)

END
OF
A
DARK
ROAD

END OF A DARK ROAD

Crystal Thrasher

A MARGARET K. MCELDERRY BOOK

Atheneum *1982* *New York*

Library of Congress Cataloging Publication Data

Thrasher, Crystal.
  End of a dark road.

  "A Margaret K. McElderry book."
  SUMMARY: In the harsh Indiana hill country during
the Depression, Seeley Robinson, her family, and her
friends share hard times and personal troubles.
  [1. Family life—Fiction. 2. Country life—Fiction.
3. Indiana—Fiction. 4. Depressions—1929—Fiction]
I. Title.
PZ7.T4En   [Fic]   82-3958
ISBN 0-689-50250-8   AACR2

Published simultaneously in Canada by McClelland & Stewart, Ltd.
Composition by American-Stratford Graphic Services, Inc.
Brattleboro, Vermont
Printed and bound by Fairfield Graphics
Fairfield, Pennsylvania
First Edition

This book is dedicated to my grandchildren

with my love.

Craig and Cathy

Christy and Baird

and Tara Lynne

END
OF
A
DARK
ROAD

chapter one

The cold wind struck me like a slap in the face as I stepped out the door, taking my breath away and whipping my thin cotton skirt around my bare legs. I turned up the collar of the blue denim jacket I had on to cover my ears and ducked my head deeper into the protection of my shoulders as I hurried up the dirt road over the ridge and down the other side of the hill to catch the school bus.

It wasn't full daylight yet, but it was light enough that I could see to dodge the ruts and chuckholes in the frozen earth road. If I watched where I was going. But I didn't. Just before I got to the gravel road where the school bus stopped for me, I stumbled and fell, breaking the thin strip of inner tube that was holding the flapping sole to my shoe.

3

"I wish I was sixteen," I grumbled aloud, as I fumbled on the ground for the piece of rubber tubing. "If I was sixteen, I would quit school right today!"

I found the strip of rubber inner tube, tied it securely around my shoe, then went on down the road. I knew I had to. I wouldn't be sixteen for nearly two years yet.

Pete Avery, the bus driver, had stopped the school bus and he was waiting for me at the end of our road. I was the first one to board the bus in the morning and the last one to leave it in the evening when we came home.

Mr. Avery said he didn't mind waiting for me in the morning. He had all day ahead of him. But, by darn, he wanted me off that bus as soon as it stopped in the evening. He wanted to get home then, to his hot supper and his chair by the fire. This last, the way he said it, sounded like his cheer by the far.

The toe of my loose shoe sole caught on the first step, and I stumbled the rest of the way into the bus where I fell into the seat directly behind the driver.

"Wake up, Seely," Pete Avery said. "We're going to have a pretty day for a change. You wouldn't want to miss it, would you?"

"Yes, I would," I replied. "I'd like to skip over every day for the next two years."

Mr. Avery was busy shifting the gears on the big bus, and he didn't say anything for a while. Then he said, "I guess your pa didn't find any work again this week." He made it sound like a question.

I shook my head no. "Dad's suppose to start working

4

on the WPA before long," I said. "The woman at the county welfare office told him last week, when he was there, that they would let him know where to report for work. But he hasn't heard from there yet."

Dad had been out of work for almost a year now. The factory where Dad had worked in Crowe had closed its doors and moved out of Greene County overnight. One week Dad was working, and the next week he was walking the floor and telling Mom not to worry. "This is nineteen hundred thirty-five," he'd said. "I'll find another job." But he hadn't. Finally, Dad had had to go to the county superintendent and ask for help to tide us over until he did find a job.

The county welfare people helped. In a left-handed kind of way. And we did all we could to help ourselves. Mom and Dad put out a big garden, using the seeds that the county provided. Mom dried and canned beans and pumpkins, and Dad hauled pumpkins to the hard road and sold them for a nickel each. Lots of them were left to rot in the garden, after we got diarrhea from eating so much pumpkin.

When it got too cold for my brother Robert to go barefoot to school in Jubilee, where he was in the second grade, Dad went to the county superintendent again. He told him that we needed shoes. Dad said later, he figured that while he was there, he would ask for shoes for the whole family. But all he got from the welfare people was a requisition slip granting the bearer no more than two pairs of shoes. Dad had argued with them, saying there were four in his family to be shod. But it hadn't done him a bit of good. Welfare said he could take it or leave it. There were many others who would be glad to get two pairs of shoes to keep their feet from the ground. Dad took the slip of paper and bought shoes for himself and Robert. The very next week, the sole came off my shoe.

A cold blast of wind jogged my mind back to here and now. I pulled my denim jacket closer around me. Mr. Avery had rolled the window down to get rid of his cud of tobacco. He wasn't allowed to smoke while he was driving the school bus, he said. So he chewed long green.

He shivered his shoulders and quickly rolled the window back up. "I've got a barn full of long green tobacco just hanging there," he said, wiping his mouth on the back of his hand. "I'd be a darn fool not to use it. But spitting into this cold wind is getting to be more than I can abide," he added.

Before I could think of a suitable answer to that, he was stopping the bus at Onalee Williams's corner to pick up Russell Williams. Her name wasn't Williams any more. It was Chally. But everyone still called the farm the Williams place. Russell's dad had been gored to death by a bull about this time last winter, and soon after the new year began, Onalee, his mother, had married the hired man, Morton Chally. Russell was fifteen and in my grade at school. He turned quiet after his dad was killed and didn't have much to say when his mother remarried. But he told me that nothing much had changed around home. The only difference he could see was that now

Morton Chally slept in the house instead of the little room off the barn. But I could see a difference in Russell.

Russell got on the bus, sat down next to me, and put his dinner bucket on the floor between his feet. He grinned at me and I saw that his face was swollen and discolored again this morning. He leaned forward and tapped Mr. Avery on the shoulder. "Don't you have any heat in here this morning?" he asked. "We're shivering so bad that we're shaking the bus."

"It'll warm up in here when we get a few more bodies aboard," Mr. Avery said. "And they'll help to hold this old bus down too," he added with a soft chuckle.

I touched Russell on the arm, and he turned his face toward me. "Did he hurt you bad this time, Russell?" I asked quietly.

He gave me a halfway grin and shook his head. "Naw," he said. "You have to like someone before they can do anything to hurt you. And he knows that I hate his guts. That's why he keeps batting me around."

"Why doesn't your mother put a stop to it?"

"Chally's got her fooled," Russell said. "She believes whatever he tells her. And he tells her that he's teaching me to box or wrestle, and she leaves him to it." He grinned again. "One of these times he's going to break my arm teaching me to wrestle. Then he'll be sorry. He'll have to do all the chores around the farm by himself."

The bus stopped to pick up more waiting kids, so we didn't talk anymore.

7

Annabel Grewe got on the bus at this stop, along with the three Knight boys and Peedle Porter. Peedle's real name was Rudolph, but I doubt if he would have answered to it. Even the teachers at school called him Peedle and never once asked why the other kids snickered every time they heard the name.

The three Knight boys went all the way to the back of the bus to sit, but Annabel and Peedle slid into the seat behind Russell and me. Their faces were red from the cold, but Peedle's got even redder when Annabel said, "Peedle, if you're going to sit here, sit closer to me so I can get warm."

Russell and I smiled at each other and turned our heads to talk to Annabel. She was in the second year of high school, same as we were, and she was always ready to talk. Even in class and study hall. Annabel was the first to tell you that she spent more time in the office, for talking out of turn, than she did in the classroom. But it didn't seem to hurt her grades. She made as good on her report card as Russell and me. And we never missed a class.

"Seely," Annabel said, "ask Avery if he is going to leave the bus parked at the store today, and if he is, can we eat our lunch in the bus. It's too cold to sit outside on those benches at school."

"I'll ask him," I said. "But I don't think he'll allow it. He's been keeping the bus locked up tighter than a drum ever since that trouble earlier this year."

Pete Avery and his wife ran the grocery store that sat on the corner from the school. Sometimes Mr. Avery

8

left the bus parked there during the day and helped his wife in the store. Last year, Annabel Grewe, Roxie Treadwell, and I ate our lunch in the school bus nearly every day and he never complained about it. Once in a while we would find three cupcakes that Mr. Avery had left for us.

But then soon after school started this year, Mr. Avery had found cigaret butts and ashes in the bus where someone had been smoking in there. Since we were the only ones he knew about who used the bus at lunchtime, Mr. Avery stopped Annabel and Roxie and me in the hall, between classes, and gave us a talking to about smoking in the school bus. We told him that we weren't the ones who were smoking. We had never touched tobacco in our lives.

He had seemed satisfied with our answer at the time. But the next day when he found that someone had been smoking in there again, Mr. Avery went to the school principal, Mr. Drayer.

Mr. Drayer called me out of class first and took me to his office. It was just a big desk in one corner of the library, but he called it his office. If anyone wanted a book from the library while Mr. Drayer was talking to one of the kids at his desk, they had to wait outside the door until he was finished or come back later. He started our talk by saying that he didn't believe I was the one who was smoking. I was too young. Besides that, he said, he doubted that I would have the money to buy cigarettes.

"But Seely, if you know who's been smoking in the

bus," he said, "and don't tell me about it, you'll be expelled from school right along with them."

I tried to look him in the eye to answer, but he kept his eyes on the pencil that he was twirling between his fingers and wouldn't look at me. "Annabel and Roxie, and sometimes Ogretta Roberts, are the only ones I run with here at school," I said, keeping my eyes on my feet and my voice low. "And they don't smoke. I don't know any girls who do," I finished lamely.

Mr. Drayer stopped all pretense of being a genial, understanding listener. His lips flattened into a thin line and he tossed the pencil he had been rolling between his fingers onto the desk with a quick flip of his wrist.

"Don't lie to me, Seely!" His voice was as low as mine, but his dark eyes were alive with anger. "I'll get your mother to come here," he said. "And I'll talk to her at the same time I speak to the mothers of the other three girls. I'll explain why I've had to expel you." He waited for me to say something—name the ones who were smoking or beg him not to expel me from classes. When I didn't speak, he said, "A fat lot of good your lying will do you when the others admit they did it."

I started crying and shaking my head. "They didn't," I said. "We've never smoked in the bus."

"Then why are you afraid to have me talk to your mother? What can she tell me that you don't want known?"

I sniffled my tears and tried to wipe my face dry with my hands. "Mom wouldn't believe me anymore than you do," I said, and started crying again.

Mr. Drayer shoved a big white handkerchief into my hands, and said, "Now hush your bawling. I'm not going to hurt you." He turned his back on me, embarrassed by my crying, and went to stare out the window at the empty playground.

I wiped my face, blew my nose into his clean handkerchief, and waited for him to dismiss me. After a while, Mr. Drayer said, "I see no reason to bother your mother with this. Do you, Seely?"

I shook my head. "No, I don't," I said to his back.

"Go back to your class now. But say nothing about this to anyone. I'll talk to the other girls later."

I mumbled, "Thank you," and laid his handkerchief on the desk and fled from the room. I washed my face at the sink in the Home Economics room, then waited there until the bell rang, dismissing school for the day.

Annabel told me later that when Mr. Drayer had talked to her and Roxie he had threatened to call their folks to the school also, but he hadn't carried through with the threat. He had talked to Pete Avery instead and afterwards, the school bus had been kept locked whenever it was left at the Averys' store.

"That was months ago," Annabel said now. "They've probably forgotten about it. When Avery stops the bus to pick up the Otis kids, you ask him anyway."

The five Otis children were the last ones to get on the bus before we got to the schoolhouse. While they were trying to find a place to sit, I leaned over Mr. Avery's shoulder and said, "Could Annabel and I eat lunch in the bus today? We'll take care not to leave crumbs on the seats."

Mr. Avery caught my eye in the long rearview mirror that ran the width of the bus. "Seely, it's all right with me if you girls want to eat in the bus. But just don't mess with my mirror."

Mirror came out sounding like he said mare, and I giggled. "We won't touch it," I promised for us all.

"See that you don't." Mr. Avery closed the bus door and drove on toward the schoolhouse. "Girls! Always primping and powdering," he muttered to himself. "And tilting my mirror, leaving fingermarks on it from one end to the other."

"You can eat in the bus," Russell told Annabel with a laugh. "But don't dare to touch Pete's mare. You leave fingermarks on it."

We were still laughing about Pete's mare when the bus pulled into the schoolyard and stopped.

chapter two

At noon, Annabel, Roxie, Ogretta Roberts, and I fought the cold wind uphill from the schoolhouse to the Averys' grocery store, where the big yellow bus was parked close to the building. We didn't try to talk until we were in the bus. The wind would have taken our breath and blown the words away before they were out of our mouths. But as soon as the bus door was closed behind us, everyone started talking at once.

"First, I'm going to warm my legs," Ogretta said. "Then I'll think about eating." She reached under her skirt, unpinned the rolled-up legs of her long underwear, and shivered with pleasure as she smoothed them down to her ankles. I pulled my bare legs up under my skirt and sat on them to warm them.

13

"Seely, you ought to wear long cotton stockings when it's this cold," Roxie said. Annabel nudged her and shook her head, and Roxie got real busy taking her lunch of two hardboiled eggs and Saltine crackers out of a brown bag and putting them on the seat next to Ogretta's peanut butter sandwich.

"I don't blame Seely," Annabel said. "I wouldn't wear those ugly cotton stockings, either."

She picked up her lunchbag and mine and started putting our food on the seat with the other stuff. I had two potatoes boiled with the jackets on, and two cold biscuits buttered in the center with margarine that hadn't been colored. Annabel had salmon patties on yeast bread in her lunch, and a man-sized hunk of eggless, butterless cake.

Annabel and Roxie knew that I wasn't vain. I would have worn any kind of stockings to keep myself warm. Even long underwear like Ogretta's if I'd had it to wear. They were just trying to save face for me. Annabel had come to my rescue last year, soon after I had started to high school, and she had been trying to take care of me ever since.

Her family had once been well-to-do people. Not wealthy, but in far better straits than the rest of us. Annabel wore cardboard in her shoes when the soles wore thin, but you'd never know it from the way they looked on the outside. And her clothes had been mended many times. These things didn't faze Annabel. She walked and acted like it didn't matter what she had on.

She was Annabel Grewe, and that was what counted. It didn't seem to bother her a whit that her three best friends wore other people's hand-me-downs and welfare clothes. The first day I had worn the denim jacket that the welfare had given us, Annabel exclaimed over it and borrowed it to wear around school all that day. No one ever made any remarks about my jacket after that.

We divided the food on the bus seat so that each of us had an equal share of the eggs and potatoes, sandwiches and cake. Then we sat huddled close in the dead cold of the bus, our teeth chattering, and talked about summer. What we would do then and later on, when we were out of school.

Ogretta said, "When I'm old enough, I'm going so far away that I'll never hear anyone laugh and say that Robertses and ragweed are taking over the county. Sometimes, I get sick to my stomach when someone asks my name. I know what they're going to say when they hear it."

"I like the name Roberts," Annabel said. "I wouldn't turn it down if it was offered to me."

Annabel had a crush on Gretta's older brother, Jay. She never missed a chance to go home with Ogretta and spend the night. Even though she knew she'd have to share a pallet on the floor with Gretta and they'd sleep cold, Annabel would go anyway.

Ogretta lived on the south end of Oolitic. Too close to the school to ride the bus, but too far away to go home for her lunch. I had never been to her house, but Gretta said it was a little, run-down shack, just bursting at the seams with Roberts kids and wall-to-wall mattresses.

"If you want to raise Robertses like rabbits," Gretta said to Annabel, "you go ahead and cabbage on to my brother, Jay. He'll see that you're satisfied."

We all giggled, and Annabel turned bright pink.

"Charlie asked me to sit in the seat right behind him this morning," Roxie said. "He kept watching me in the rearview mirror, and once he smiled and winked at me."

Roxie Treadwell lived back in the hills around Guthrie and rode Charlie Buskirk's bus to school. She didn't go on about Charlie quite as much now as she had last year, but we knew she was still stuck on him. Now that Charlie Buskirk had finally noticed Roxie, we'd have to listen to her sing his praises all over again.

"Roxie, Charlie Buskirk is old enough to be your dad," Annabel said. "He don't mean nothing with his smiles and his winks."

Gretta giggled. "Miss Hendricks would have a fit if she ever heard you make a statement like that in English class."

Annabel shrugged her shoulders. "Well, he doesn't," she said, smiling at Gretta. "And Roxie is going to get in trouble if she pays any attention to him. Charlie would say it was like taking candy from a baby," she added quietly.

"Well, I'm not a baby," Roxie said, tossing her long, dark hair. "I'll be sixteen next month and I can go with Charlie Buskirk if I want to."

16

Ogretta put her arm around Roxie and pulled her closer to our huddle. "You've wanted to for a year, Roxie," she said. "It wasn't your age that held you back. It was Charlie. He has never asked you."

Roxie smiled sheepishly. "But he will," she said, sure of herself. "You'll see."

"Not today, we won't," Annabel said. "There's the three minute bell. We've got to get going."

Gretta started rolling up her long underwear and looking for the pins that held the legs securely under her skirt. I cleared away all signs of our lunch and wiped the seat clean with the wadded brown bags. Annabel and Roxie stretched their necks to see in Mr. Avery's rearview mirror while they powdered and put on lip rouge. When they were finished, they wet their fingers with spit and brushed their eyelashes and smoothed the powder from their eyebrows. "We're ready," Roxie said. "Let's get these bodies back to school."

The sharp, cutting wind was at our backs going down the hill to the schoolhouse and we could talk without having the words snatched away by the wind as soon as they were spoken. Ogretta and I were walking behind Roxie and Annabel, our arms around each other for warmth.

"Seely, you haven't mentioned Byron Tyson in ages," Gretta said. "Aren't you still writing to him?"

"I send notes to him in with Aunt Fanny's letters," I said. "But she doesn't write very often. I guess his classes at college are keeping him pretty busy. He never writes to me," I added quietly.

Gretta smiled and squeezed my arm encouragingly. "He'll be home for Thanksgiving," she said. "Then everything will be just as it was before he ever went to Vincennes."

"I hope so."

The last bell rang as we entered the building and we split up, each one going to her next class or homeroom. I didn't have a class the first period of the afternoon, so I went to study hall to prepare for second period Ancient History class. I got out my book, but I couldn't keep my mind on my studying.

I wished that I could be as sure as Ogretta was that Byron would be home, and unchanged, at Thanksgiving. Gretta didn't know as well as I did how college could turn a person around. My sister, Julie, had left home a year and a half ago to attend normal college in Terre Haute, and we hadn't seen her since.

But Julie wrote to us regularly. Dad said that he could understand how it was with Julie. She needed every penny she could lay her hands on for her education. She couldn't afford to come home. He said even working at two jobs, the college cafeteria during the day and as a waitress at night, Julie was barely making ends meet.

But Mom argued that going off to college had changed Julie. She could come home if she wanted to, Mom said. But Julie thought she was better than the rest of us now.

Maybe Byron Tyson would think that he was too good to have a friend like me, I thought. No doubt, now that he was a college student, I would seem really dumb to him.

He seemed to have outgrown me even before he had left for college. The few times that I'd seen Byron last summer, he never seemed to have any time for me. He had worked at the Spring Mill State Park all summer and he'd seldom been home. Then in late August, just before he went to Vincennes, Byron had spent two whole days with his dad and Aunt Fanny Phillips. For those two days we were together almost all the time, and Byron was the dear friend I'd come to depend on.

We went to see the Reverend Mr. Paully and his wife, Nellie, on the last afternoon Byron was at home. We stayed to eat supper with them and walked home later by the woods path.

"I feel like this is Johnny's and my track through the woods," Byron said. "And I never come this way that I don't feel like Johnny is walking here beside me."

"I know," I said quietly. "I'm always being reminded of Johnny by one thing or another."

Johnny Meaders had been a good friend to Byron Tyson a lot longer than he'd been my best friend, but when Nellie Fender's two backward boys killed Johnny, I grieved for him the same as Byron. Nellie Fender was Mrs. Paully now, and we didn't talk about her boys. But we hadn't forgotten Schylar and Sylvester and what they did to Johnny.

The late evening breeze moved the branches of the hazelnut thicket ahead of us and made shadows across the path, like swift moving beings, skipping from one side of the path to the other.

"I still keep expecting to see Schylar and Sylvester

19

Fender skulking and sneaking through these woods, waiting to cause us trouble." Goose pimples rose on my arms and a shiver ran down my spine. "I'm glad they're locked up where they can't touch us," I added.

We walked in silence for the next few minutes, each absorbed with our own thoughts. Then Byron said, "I'm glad that Nellie Fender married the preacher."

"So am I," I said. "Nellie deserves a good life, after what she went through with Schylar and Sylvester."

Byron kind of laughed. "You know, Seely, after they were put away and Nellie took it so well, I figured that we were the ones who had helped her through the bad times. But I was wrong. We might have helped a little, but it was Mr. Paully who really did the most for her."

I thought to myself, They had helped each other. Just as Byron and I had helped each other adjust to the loss of Johnny.

We had sat on the porch steps at my house that night and talked the moon up and over the treetops, leaving the porch in deep shadow. Even then, Byron seemed reluctant to leave. It was as if he knew that things would never quite be the same between us. That the next time we met we'd both be changed by time, and we'd feel differently about each other.

Now as I turned to the middle of the book and started reading the assignment for Ancient History class, I hoped that Byron wouldn't change too much. Maybe if I studied real hard, I thought, and learned everything I could, Byron wouldn't find me too dull to have for a friend.

When the bell rang for class, I gathered up my books and pages full of scribbled notes on Alexander the Great and joined the group that was leaving the study hall for History class.

chapter three

Miss Hendricks stopped me as I was leaving the building that evening to ask me about a short story that I had turned in for a class assignment a few days earlier. "Seems to me that I've read something very similar to your story," she said. She fussed with the papers and books that she held clasped to her bosom and wouldn't look at me while she spoke.

"Maybe you did," I said. "I got the idea from an old newspaper article that told about a woman who won a hog-calling contest."

Miss Hendricks shook her head. "No, I don't believe that was where I read it," she said. Then she asked, "I don't suppose you could bring the item in to class with you so I could see it?"

I said sure, I'd be glad to. "It was in an old paper that

Linzy Meaders sent to Mom from Pikeville, Kentucky. She won't mind if I bring it to school."

Before she could detain me further, I said, "I've got to go now, Miss Hendricks. I'll miss my bus home." I turned and hurried as fast as I could down the hall and out the front door.

Even by hurrying, when I got to the bus all the seats were taken near the front and I had to go almost to the last row of seats to find a place to sit.

Peedle Porter was sitting with Annabel Grewe and he jumped up when he saw me and said, "Sit here, Seely. I was saving this seat for you."

I sat down next to Annabel. Peedle stood close beside me and held to the back of my seat to steady himself against the sudden lurching and jarring of the school bus. For some reason that I didn't know about, there were quite a few extra people riding the bus this evening and the aisle was crowded with the ones who couldn't find a seat.

Elsworth Starnes and Jummy Lewis, both seniors who played on the basketball team and ran track, always had a place to sit. But this evening they were standing in the aisle behind Peedle Porter. They snickered when Peedle got up and gave me his seat. Then they started nudging and shoving Peedle and singing, "Peedle's got a girlfriend. Peedle's stuck on Seely Robinson," and getting everyone else to laugh at him.

I felt my dander rising, but when Peedle ignored them, I let it pass also. Annabel said that it was just as well that we did. "If you make a fuss about it," she whis-

23

pered, "they will get worse and keep it up all the way home."

We hadn't reached the Otises' stop when Elsworth Starnes grabbed Peedle by the back of his sweater and said, "I'm talking to you, Porter. You pay attention when I speak and answer me."

"I didn't hear you," Peedle said. "What did you say?"

Elsworth gave Peedle's sweater a jerk, nearly pulling it off his back. "I asked you what your old lady was wearing today," he said. "The last time I saw her, she had on this sweater."

Jummy Lewis snickered. "I'll bet I know. They both own a dirty gray sweater that's raveled out at the elbows."

They both laughed as Peedle tried to pull free of them and wrap his sweater closer around himself. But they weren't ready to give up teasing him yet. Jummy Lewis caught a loose thread that was dangling from the hole in the sleeve and gave it a hard pull. When he and Elsworth finished unraveling the sweater sleeve, there was just a short stub of knit tubing still attached to the shoulder piece of the sweater.

"They're ruined Mom's good sweater," Peedle said, and he looked like he wanted to cry.

I called to Mr. Avery and told him what they were doing to Peedle Porter, and I said it loud and clear. But I guess with all the commotion that was going on on the bus, Mr. Avery didn't hear me. But the ones who were tormenting Peedle heard me, and after that they started pestering me.

24

"Seely's stuck on Peedle or she wouldn't be sticking up for him," Jummy Lewis said. Then Elsworth Starnes took it from there, adding words that shouldn't have been said any place, let alone on a school bus where all the kids could hear them. "Maybe Seely would like to have Peedle on her lap," he said, and gave Peedle a hard shove toward me.

Peedle landed on his knees in the aisle beside me, his head and shoulders in my lap and his arms clutched around my knees for support. It wasn't true what they had said about me and Peedle. I didn't have a crush on him. Had anyone asked me earlier, I would have said that I didn't even like Peedle Porter. But I wasn't going to sit still and watch while someone mistreated him.

I pushed him away as gently as I could and got up. "Get up, Peedle," I said quietly. "You can sit here beside Annabel and I'll stand in the aisle."

Annabel tried to stop me. She said, "Don't do it, Seely. You'll get hurt."

I looked straight into Elsworth Starnes's grinning face and told Annabel, "If anyone even dares to touch me, I'll knock his block off."

I only said that because I knew they wouldn't be able to keep their hands off me. Not after I had practically dared them to touch me. And I wanted them to. When Elsworth Starnes so much as laid a finger on me, I was going to shame him so bad in front of his friends that he would never want to show his face on this bus again. And I knew just how to do it, too.

One day last summer when Aunt Fanny Phillips had

25

been at our house helping Mom can green beans, and I was sitting on the back porch breaking the beans, I heard Aunt Fanny tell Mom that a piano salesman had stopped at the Starnes place and Mavis Starnes had left home with him. She was gone for two weeks—in Louisville, Aunt Fanny said—and she came back home with a baby grande piano. "That's not bad wages for two weeks work." She laughed and added, "And to think Mavis didn't even have to get out of bed to earn it."

Mom had clucked her tongue and said, "A body would have to want a piano mighty bad to do something like that." And Aunt Fanny had replied, "She did. Mighty bad."

Peedle wiped his nose on his shirt sleeve and scooted over closer to Annabel. "There's room for you, too, Seely."

I shook my head. "That's all right, Peedle. I'll stand."

Just as I had expected, I felt a tug at the tail of my jacket, as soon as I turned my back on Elsworth Starnes. I pretended that I hadn't noticed it. The next tug was so strong that it nearly jerked me off my feet. I pulled my jacket free and whirled to face Elsworth. He took a step back from me.

"Peedle Porter's mother and mine don't know any traveling salesmen," I flared out at Elsworth. "So we have to make do with what we have. But one thing we don't have to do is to put up with the likes of you!"

Elsworth raised his eyebrows and assumed his superior look. "And what's that suppose to mean?" he asked.

"Suppose you ask your mother, if you don't already

know," I answered. "I'm sure she must have gotten more than just a piano from that man in Louisville."

"You keep your mouth shut about my mother!" He raised his hand to hit me, and I elbowed him hard in the stomach: knocking him backward into the line of standing passengers. There was a great rush of grabbing for seat backs as they lost their balance on the bumpy bus and falling in the aisle when they missed. I had started a chain reaction when I hit Elsworth Starnes that just wouldn't stop.

But the bus could. And did. Mr. Avery got out of the driver's seat and came storming toward the rear of the bus, his face like a stormcloud. I had never seen him so angry. And it frightened me.

In the mass of confusion I was the only one standing quietly by myself, so Mr. Avery addressed his questions to me.

"Seely, what in the name of heaven is going on here? What started this . . . this landslide?"

"I did," I said, my voice so low that I could barely hear it. "But it wasn't in the name of heaven. More like the other place, if you ask me."

"Well, I'm asking you!" He was losing his temper and his patience with me. "And you'd better tell me, right here and now!"

I tried to start at the beginning, to tell him how it all began, but he waved his hand at me and said, "Never mind, just get on with it." So I said, "I hit Elsworth in the belly and knocked him into the rest of them, and they fell down."

By this time, everyone was shouting and shoving and trying to tell Mr. Avery their side of it. But he shouted them down.

"I won't stand for any roughhousing on my school bus," he said. "And anybody that can't abide by that rule can get out and walk." He turned to me and said, "Seely, apologize to Elsworth and let's get the rest of these younguns on home."

I clamped my lips shut and shook my head no.

"Then say you're sorry for fighting," Mr. Avery humored me. "Otherwise, you'll have to walk home."

"All right. I'll walk. But I won't ever apologize to Elsworth Starnes for anything." I reached to take my books from Peedle Porter and leave the bus. "I'll carry your things for you," Peedle said, and slid out of the seat and followed me down the aisle and off the bus.

Russell Williams tried to leave the bus with us, but Mr. Avery told Russell to sit down and behave himself. "I'm not looking to have trouble with your stepdaddy," he said. "You'll stay on this bus and get out at home where he expects you." Mr. Avery closed the bus door and drove on, leaving Peedle Porter and me standing alongside the road. We were more than five miles from home, and dark was coming on fast.

We had ridden the bus together for more than a year, but I still didn't really know Peedle. Only what I had heard others say about him. So I didn't know what to expect from him. Last year when I had asked Annabel Grewe why they called him Peedle, she told me that he would unbutton and pee wherever the urge struck him,

28

no matter who was there at the time. "That's why they call him Peedle," she had said. "He don't know no better than a baby."

But that evening as he walked with me he made no move to relieve himself. Mostly, he tried to keep between me and the cold wind, hugging the ragged sweater close across his thin chest and hurrying to keep up with me. When we came to the dirt lane that led up the hollow to his house, he said, "Seely, would you like to come home with me and get warm?"

"I'd better keep going, Peedle. Mom will be out beating the bushes for me the way it is."

His face was blue with cold, but he grinned anyway and lifted a hand in farewell. "Sure," he said. "See you tomorrow." He bent into the wind and started on up the hollow.

"I'll see you," I called after him. "And thanks, Peedle, for walking with me." He didn't answer, but he lifted his hand and waved to let me know he had heard me.

It was full dark when I passed the Williams place. Even the house was all dark except for a dim light in one room at the back of the house. When I turned the corner, heading toward Jubilee and home, I saw a light in the barnyard, like someone carrying a lantern. Probably Russell, I thought, just now finishing up the chores and going inside to eat his supper.

Supper would be over by the time I got home. I figured that Mom was more than likely worrying her head off about me right now. But I knew from experience that as soon as I walked through the door, safe and sound, she would be mad as a hornet and ready to beat me to death for worrying her so. That's the way Mom was. She could be worried sick about Dad if he didn't come home when he had said he'd be there. But the minute he walked in and she saw that he was all in one piece, she lit into him like a buzz saw.

I just hoped that this would be one of the times that Mom would take her angry relief out in words. As cold as my legs were tonight, I couldn't bear a switching. Every so often I stopped and hunkered down, letting my skirt warm my legs for a moment before going on. But the warmth didn't last long. In just a few minutes they would be stinging and tingling with cold again.

The moon came up, casting weird shadows across the road ahead of me, where I had to pass to get home. Once I thought I saw someone crouching at the side waiting to spring out at me, but then the wind moved the brush and I saw that it was only a shadow.

"Next time, I'll say I'm sorry," I told myself "even to Elsworth Starnes, before I'll walk home in the dark." But even while I was saying it, I knew I wouldn't do it. I hunkered down and warmed my legs for a moment, then when my heart was beating normally again after the fright I'd had from the shadow, I stood up and hurried on my way again.

I had my head drawn down between my shoulders, covering my face and ears from the cold with my jacket, so I nearly walked on by the dirt road that led back to our house. I was glad to get to it. Even frozen solid like it was, it was easier to walk on than the gravel. The piece of rubber tubing that had held my shoe sole all day, had worn through and fallen off after I'd left the bus. If I didn't watch how I stepped, the flapping sole would bend under my shoe and I would have no protection from the gravel road. As bad as I hated to do it, I would have to tell Dad about my shoes tonight. There was no way that he could get new shoes for me, but maybe he could fix them so they would last a little longer.

Dad was going to be mad, probably madder than Mom, because I had caused a commotion on the bus and Mr. Avery had made me walk home. I hoped that they would give me a chance to tell them what had happened before they started asking me a lot of questions, I thought, as I opened the gate and went up the path to the kitchen door. So many times, I never got to open my mouth. And when I did, Mom said I was sassing her or not paying attention like I should. I opened the door and walked into the warm kitchen. Mom came from the front room and started toward me. "Just don't switch my legs," I begged. "I don't think I could stand it." And I started crying.

Mom said, "There. There, now. Hush your crying. You're home." She put her arm around me and pulled me over to the cookstove. "Stand here a minute and get warm, while I bring you a chair and something hot to drink."

I stayed where she put me, but I couldn't stop crying. The heat from the stove made my hands and legs hurt as much as the cold had. Mom brought a chair and sat me down. Then she knelt, took off my shoes, and began to rub my feet.

"Rob," she raised her voice to call Dad. "You'd better come here and look at this youngun's feet and legs. I think they're frostbitten."

Dad came to the kitchen carrying a wool blanket in his arms like he was cuddling a baby. "I've been keeping this blanket near the fire," he said. "I figured you'd need something to warm you when you got home." He spread the blanket over my knees, but then he seemed at a loss about what to do with the rest of it. "Seely, take off that jacket and let me wrap this around your shoulders."

I couldn't manage the buttons on my jacket. There was no feeling in my fingers. Mom got the jacket off me, then the two of them wrapped the warm blanket around my feet and legs and pulled one end of it up to cover my head.

"You'll be all right," Dad said, as he lapped the corners of the blanket over my chest. "Soon as you're thawed out your mother will fix you some hot supper."

"I was scared," I said, just above a whisper. "I thought you'd be mad when I didn't come home on the bus."

"We would've been," Dad said, "had the bus driver not come here and explained to us about what was keeping you."

Mom broke in to say, "Mr. Avery told us that he hated to do it. But if he made an exception of you, he'd never be able to make his word stand for anything on that bus."

"From the way he told it," she went on, "he figures

that most everyone knows that he favors you. And if he would make you get off the bus and walk home, then he'd not hesitate to put anyone on the road who caused him any trouble."

Dad cleared his throat to let Mom know that he had something to say about it now. I looked at him and I knew from the serious and sober set of his face that I was about to get the only punishment I would receive for fighting on the school bus and worrying them. And I knew also that I deserved more than I would get.

"We're letting this pass, this time," Dad said. "Seeing as how it wasn't your doing at the start. But don't let me ever hear tell of you fighting again. A girl your age ought to be able to reason her way out of an argument," he added quietly, "and not have to resort to fighting like a roughneck."

"Yes, sir," I said softly. Then I blurted, "But he made me so mad!"

Dad frowned at me. "We'll hear no more about it," he said. "Now eat your supper and get to bed. Morning will be here before you're ready."

I didn't understand Mom and Dad's unexpected kindness, but I didn't question it. I ate supper and went to bed as I was told, and I slept all night wrapped in the wool blanket that Dad had warmed for me. My last thought was that I had forgotten to tell Dad that my shoes needed fixing.

chapter four

"Seely, get up!" Mom called. "It's six o'clock. You'll miss the school bus!"

She said the same thing every morning. Sometimes, I would lie in bed thinking that I'd catch her up short. But no matter whether I leaped out of bed at once or waited for the second or third call before I got up, it was always six o'clock right on the dot when I got to the kitchen.

This morning I jumped out of bed, gathered up my clothes, and went to the front room, where it was warm, to get dressed. I found my shoes sitting near the stove, all cleaned and polished, with new laces. Dad had put half-soles on them while I slept and cut and fitted leather pieces over the worn, runover heels to make them stand level.

I put on my shoes and pulled the laces tight to tie

34

them. They felt good, snug and straight on my feet, almost like new shoes. I finished dressing, then went to the kitchen to thank Dad for fixing them for me.

Mom was adding flour to the bacon grease to make gravy for breakfast. Dad was no where in sight. "Gus Tyson came by for your dad near an hour ago," Mom said, when I asked where he was. "Your dad got word by mail yesterday that he was to pick up a work order this morning for a job on the WPA, working for the county. Gus drove him over to get it," she added.

"I just wanted to tell Dad that my shoes look and feel just like new," I said.

Mom only nodded, then went on stirring the gravy. "You'd better get your brother up for school," she said. "Then come and eat your breakfast. It will be daylight soon."

Robert was out of bed already. He had on an old slip-over sweater and a pair of patched overalls, and he was trying to pull his good overalls on over them. "Robert, you can't do that," I told him.

"Yes, I can," he said, his face set and stubborn. "If you'll hold onto the legs of the first pair so they won't creep up, I can get these others on over them."

To humor him, I held the cuffs of the ragged pants while he pulled on his good overalls. He buttoned a flannel shirt over the old sweater, then fastened his overall galluses over it all. When he was finished, I told him that he looked like a stuffed sausage and I doubted that he could even bend over to tie his shoes. But he proved me wrong by stooping to fold the first pair of overall legs inside his sox, then stringing up his shoes and tying them over the bulky wad. "Now, I'll be warm," he said, as he stood up to leave the room.

"I got cold yesterday," Robert said, keeping his voice low, as if he didn't want Mom to hear him. "And, Seely, I never did get warm. Not even after I got to the schoolhouse."

I looked at his serious, wide blue eyes, too serious for such a young face, and assured him that he would be warm today. "No wind could possibly get through all those clothes," I said, and pushed him gently toward the kitchen and our breakfast.

I only had to walk to the gravel road, then I could get on the bus and out of the cold. But Robert had to walk all the way to Jubilee to school. Last year, he would sometimes stop at Nellie Fender's to get warm, but I never heard him mention stopping there any more.

Robert and I left the house at the same time this morning. I watched as he struck off across the field toward the woods and the path that passed by Nellie's house. Nellie lived on the pike road, just this side of Jubilee, but we had made a shortcut to her house that lopped off quite a bit of the way there. Then I turned and started up the dirt road to catch the school bus to Oolitic. The wind didn't seem to be so cold and sharp as it had been lately, or maybe I just didn't notice it so much this morning because I had on solid shoes and a warm cap on my head.

Mom had gotten Jamie's blue stocking cap out of the

trunk that held her treasures and told me to wear it today. Jamie had been dead for more than two years now, and this was the first time his things had been touched. "It's foolish to let this good cap go to waste," Mom said, as she put it on me and pulled it down over my ears. "Jamie would want you to wear it and keep off the cold."

Maybe that was the reason I felt so good about going to school today. It had been Jamie's cap that kept my head warm when we used to walk to grade school together, and now that I was in high school, his blue stocking cap was keeping me warm again. I didn't have a cap then, either. He used to give me his to wear as soon as we were out of sight from home.

Pete Avery's school bus was waiting for me where the dirt road met the gravel. Until I saw it sitting there, I hadn't give a thought to how I would greet him this morning. We hadn't ever had any problems before now. And I didn't hold any hard feelings about the one we'd had. But I didn't know how he would feel toward me from now on.

Mr. Avery opened the bus door, and a blast of hot air hit me as I stepped onto the bus. I took my regular seat behind him and let the warm air blow directly to my bare legs. He didn't say anything, and neither did I.

After a while, when the bus was well on its way, I said, "Mr. Avery, that heat sure feels good."

He caught my eye in the overhead mirror and grinned. "I figured that it would," he said. "I left a little early on purpose just to warm the bus up for you." He kind of chuckled to let me know that he was joshing me. I smiled to say I understood.

Farther on down the road, Mr. Avery said, "Seely, I didn't like to put you off the bus, but you left me no other course to follow. Why didn't you just tell me that you were sorry for shoving Elsworth and for what you said about his ma? Then I could've overlooked it and let you stay on the bus."

"But I wasn't sorry, Mr. Avery. I aimed to hurt Elsworth Starnes any way I could. It's not fair that those bullies can pick on Peedle Porter and make fun of him and nothing's ever done about it." I was getting mad again, just thinking about it. "They ruined Peedle's sweater," I added. "And now he won't have a thing to wear."

Mr. Avery rolled down the window, got rid of his cud of tobacco, and wiped his mouth. "Don't fret yourself about the Porter boy," he said. "He's got a decent coat for school now.

"I think I'll talk to Mr. Drayer about the Starnes boy," he went on, "and let him handle that end of it. I'm going to make it plain to the principal that, from now on, no one but my regular younguns are going to board this bus. If Starnes and Lewis want a gang at their place to go coon hunting, they'll have to find another way to get there. That should get rid of the troublemakers," he added. "All but two. And we'll have to put up with Elsworth Starnes and Jummy Lewis until they graduate, or their folks run them off from home."

38

When the bus stopped at the Williams place, Russell was trotting from the barn with a pail of milk in each hand, headed for the house. A minute later, he ran out the front door swinging his dinner bucket in one hand and his schoolbooks in the other. Mr. Avery shook his head. "That boy has got his hands full in more ways than one," he observed quietly.

Yet when Russell Williams clambered onto the bus and dropped into the seat beside me, Pete Avery said, "Son, if you don't quit dillydallying and get a move on in the mornings, I'm going to have to leave you behind. I've got a sked-yule to keep, you know."

Russell just grinned at Avery's back and set his dinner bucket on the floor between his feet. Once that was done, Russell leaned back in the seat and took a long, deep breath of air, as if this was the first he'd had time to breathe since he woke up.

"Did you catch hell when you got home last night?" he asked me.

I shook my head, then answered him in a whisper so Mr. Avery wouldn't hear what I said. "Pete Avery went to the house and told Mom and Dad why I wasn't on the bus," I said. "I think he must have stretched the truth a bit when he told it. They had a warm blanket waiting when I got home and not one word of blame for me."

"I wanted to walk the rest of the way home with you," Russell said. "I hurried and got my chores done and was watching for you. But Chally saw that I was finished with my work and found other things for me to do. It

39

was way past dark by then," he added, "and I never did see you go by our house."

Peedle Porter was the first one to board the bus at the next stop. He had on a plaid mackinaw jacket that was two sizes too big for him, and a wide smile for Mr. Avery. He would've said something to Mr. Avery, but he waved Peedle on by with a curt, "Sit down somewhere, Peedle. You're letting all the heat out that open door." Peedle turned red and slid into the seat behind me, and Annabel took the one next to him.

"Seely." Peedle tapped me on the shoulder. "Seely, did Pete Avery talk to your folks last night?" He stopped and waited until I nodded my head. "He came to our house too," Peedle said. "He told Ma that he was giving me this good mackinaw for doing him a favor. Do you know what that favor was, Seely?" I shook my head this time. "He said it was for keeping an eye on you and seeing that you got to our lane safe and sound. And I did that, didn't I, Seely?"

I turned in my seat to face Peedle. "No one could've taken better care," I told him, remembering how he tried to shield me from the wind. "I hope your ma didn't blame you for what the boys did to her sweater."

It seemed to me that no matter who or what was at fault, when anything went wrong us kids were always held responsible, and in one way or another we were made to account for it. But I found out that wasn't the case at Peedle Porter's house.

He said, "Naw. Ma didn't get upset over that old sweater. She just sat down and started knitting on a new sleeve. It's not the same color, but she said it would be just as warm as the one that came on it."

Annabel giggled and nudged Peedle in the ribs with her elbow. "How come you've never seen me safely home, Peedle?" she teased him.

"You don't need anyone to look after you," Peedle said. "And besides, you're older than me."

Annabel made a pout at him, as if she was mad, and moved to the edge of the seat.

Russell laughed. "Don't fret, Annabel," he told her. "You're not too old for me."

Our feeling of warmth and well-being lasted all the way to the schoolhouse. The bus made its usual stops and waited for the same ones who were always late, but no one mentioned the trouble we'd had on the bus the night before, even when Elsworth Starnes and Jummy Lewis got on. If I hadn't known better, I would've thought that nothing had ever happened.

At the schoolhouse, Mr. Avery shut off the motor, got out of the driver's seat, and stood facing the rear of the bus. "All of you just stay in your seats for a minute," he said. "I've got something to say to you before you leave the bus."

There were moans and groans from most of the kids, but no one moved from their seats.

"Starting now, this minute," Mr. Avery said, "there will be no one allowed to ride this bus unless they live on my route. There'll be no more of this bringing two or three friends with you and having them taking up seats that my regular riders should have."

41

"Bull—loney!" Jummy Lewis shouted from the back of the bus. "I've got friends coming home with me tonight."

"Not on this bus!" Pete Avery stated firmly. "I'm going to speak to the school principal while I'm here this morning," Mr. Avery went on. "I want him to know that anyone who causes trouble on this bus will be put off along the road, and they can walk to school. It will be up to Mr. Drayer to handle it from there on."

This time, when Mr. Avery stopped speaking, no one said a word. He waited a moment, then he opened the school bus door and stepped to one side. We filed past him and off the bus.

I was in second period English class when there was a knock at the door, and a moment later, Miss Hendricks told me that I was to go to the principal's office. "Take your books with you," she said. "You won't be coming back to class today. Class will be over by the time you're through in there."

Mr. Drayer was busily writing at his desk in one corner of the library. I said, "Did you want to see me?" He barely glanced my way. "Sit over there, Seely. I'll talk to you later. After I've had a word or two with Elsworth." And he went back to his writing.

I said, "Yes sir," and moved across the room to a table by the window. It was colder near the windows, but it was the only place in the library where it was light enough to read. I opened my English textbook and started studying the day's lesson.

I don't know how long I had been sitting there when I noticed the cold and the silence of the room. I hadn't heard Mr. Drayer leave, but he was gone and the library door was closed. I got up and went to stand by the heat register, but I guess it was closed too. It wasn't any warmer there than it was by the window. I looked at the shelves of books, some with author's names that I couldn't pronounce, but I didn't touch them.

Finally, I went back to the table where I had been studying, and stood there looking out the window at the playground.

There were perhaps a dozen men or more hacking and digging at the frozen ground with picks and shovels. I watched as one man drove his pick into the hillside, breaking out frozen chunks of earth, while another scooped them up with a shovel and filled the wheelbarrow that sat waiting. Another man grasped the handles of the wheelbarrow and pushed it to the far side of the playground and dumped the dirt into a deep gulley there.

I had been watching the way the men did their work, yet not really seeing the men who did it. Then I saw Dad. He was one of the men wielding a pick near the building. He had on his sheepskin coat, and his cap was pulled low over his face. But his big bare hands were purple from the cold.

I noticed then that some of the men wore gloves. But most of them had pulled old brown and white work socks over their hands to keep off the cold. Dad was the only one I saw who didn't have some kind of cover for his hands. Every time he raised the pick and brought it down against the hard ground, I expected to see his hands break in pieces like the frozen earth.

I didn't know what I could do, but I had to do something. I could not bear to see him freezing his hands just to keep a job of work that wouldn't pay him enough to buy a week's groceries.

I left the library, put on my jacket and stocking cap, and left the schoolhouse. I knew I would be in big trouble if I was caught leaving the school, but I had to try to get a pair of gloves for Dad.

Tears were frozen on my face when I walked into Averys' general store and told Mrs. Avery that I wanted a pair of men's work gloves. "Do you ever let anything go without first getting the money?" I asked her.

"That's the way most things leave this store," she replied kindly.

"Then I'll take these," I said.

I had picked out the biggest, warmest-looking gloves she had in the store. And if she hadn't let me take them on time, I intended to steal them. Just take them and run to the playground with them.

"My dad is working," I said. "He'll pay you on payday."

Mrs. Avery gave me a slip of paper that said I owed her thirty-nine cents. I took the gloves and held them as if they were worth their weight in gold and hurried back to the schoolyard.

I'll never forget the look Dad gave me when I touched his arm and offered the gloves to him. A wide smile spread across his face, and he said, "What's this, Sis? Gloves for your old dad?" He didn't ask me how I came by them. He just accepted them.

He tucked the new gloves under one arm, blew on his hands and rubbed them together to get the blood circulating, then he slipped on the gloves. I guess it was the cold wind that was whistling across the playground that brought water to Dad's eyes. He had to wipe them before he could lift the pick and go back to work.

I had just gotten back to the office when Mr. Drayer came rushing into the room. "Good Lord, Seely! Are you still here?" He rubbed his eyes as if he couldn't believe it. "I forgot all about you," he said. "I wanted to talk to you about that trouble on the school bus last night," he added, "but that can wait now." He motioned toward the door, waving me out of the room. I went, happy to be let off so easily.

chapter five

Ogretta Roberts met me just outside the principal's office. "Seely, where have you been? We've been looking all over for you." She took my arm and headed down the steps toward the gymnasium and the locker room. "We've got your lunch sack already," Ogretta said. Annabel and Roxie are waiting for us in the furnace room. We are going to eat in there today."

I knew there had to be a furnace to keep the schoolhouse heated, but it never occurred to me that there would be a special room to house it. "It's just around the next corner," Gretta said. "But if there's anyone in the hall, we'll walk on by the door and wait till they've gone. No one is supposed to go in the furnace room," she added.

We had gone down so many halls and turned so many corners that I felt like I was lost in a subterranean tunnel and I'd never see natural light again. Then we turned the next corner and I saw a door to the outside ahead of us and I felt better about it.

"In here," Gretta said. She opened a door in the side wall and drew me quickly inside a dark, cavernous room and around the coal furnace toward a faint light at the rear of the room. Annabel and Roxie were behind the furnace. A bare light bulb dangled from the ceiling by a long cord and lit up the long wooden bench where they sat and waited for us.

I was surprised at the size of the room that had been left behind the furnace, for no purpose that I could see, and the cleanliness of it. "How did you ever find this place?" I asked, amazed.

"Roxie heard about it," Annabel answered, with a sidelong glance at Roxie. "Charlie Buskirk asked her to meet him here during last period today."

I turned to Roxie. "You're not going to, are you?"

"I might," she said. "I don't have any class to go to, and we're the only ones who'd know about it."

Annabel and Ogretta were opening lunch sacks and putting out the food on one end of the bench. They didn't seem to be paying the least attention to Roxie and me.

"But what if the janitor came in and found you here, Roxie? You would be expelled from school. And besides that," I argued, "you don't know what Charlie Buskirk might try to do, once he got you alone down here."

47

"I'm not afraid of what Charlie might do," Roxie said. "I can take care of myself."

Annabel said, "Seely, come and eat your lunch. I've talkèd till I'm blue in the face and I can't change her mind."

I took Roxie's arm, and we went together to get our share of the pooled lunches.

Ogretta gave me one fourth of a bacon sandwich and half of a boiled egg and handed the other half egg and quarter sandwich to Roxie. "Eat hardy," she said. "If we get caught in here, it's bread and water for the rest of the term. If anyone can bring the bread."

We laughed, and Roxie said, "You don't have to worry about getting caught. Charlie says that no one ever comes in here."

I wondered who kept the room so clean, if no one ever came in here. The floor was swept and the bench dusted, as if it was done every day.

"Why did Dracula keep you in the office so long?" Annabel poked me in the back. "Stop dreaming, Seely. I'm trying to pump you about what went on in the principal's office this morning."

"Nothing," I said. "He left the room and forgot that I was there. I think he went to talk to Elsworth Starnes. He looked pretty confused when he came back to the office."

Ogretta smiled. "That Elsworth could confuse anybody," she said.

The three minute bell rang. We cleaned up our crumbs and papers, waited until the hall was clear, then left the furnace room. As we separated to go to our different rooms, I said to Roxie, "Don't meet Charlie just because he asked you to. Think about it awhile."

"I have thought about it," she said, not meeting my eyes. "If I'm not there to meet him, he won't ask me again."

She turned and hurried down the hall. I went to study hall and opened my Ancient History book. There wasn't a thing in there that could help me cope with today. Mr. Yoho, our history teacher, told us that we learned from past history how to live and survive today. But so far, I hadn't found out a thing that I could use. I leafed through the book, looking at the pictures and reading the captions below them. If they'd had a depression back in those days, they sure kept it a secret. And if there were love-starved fifteen-year-old girls in the world then, they didn't rate any space in the history books. Not any more than they would here and now, I thought. And tried to dismiss Roxie from my mind and get my assignment done.

I didn't see Roxie again that day. Usually we found time at the last recess to plan something for the next day or talk over our class assignment and homework. But Roxie didn't show up. We other three didn't have much to say, either. I guess we all had our minds on what was taking place in the furnace room, but we didn't know what to do about it.

When school was out and I went to get on the school bus, Pete Avery was standing by the door to the bus giving everyone the eye as they got on. He stopped

Jummy Lewis and made him wait until everyone else was seated before he let him through the door. Jummy's friends swaggered about for a moment, then left. Pete Avery got on the bus then and closed the door. There wasn't any trouble on the bus that night. I guess Elsworth and Jummy figured that Mr. Avery meant business and wouldn't stand for any foolishness today.

Robert was carrying in the firewood when I got to the house. He always beat me home by a good hour and a half, but he usually waited for me to help him carry in the wood and water for the night. I went to the woodpile before I went into the house and loaded my arms with the big pieces of wood that Dad used to bank the fire in the front room.

Robert looked at me and smiled. "Hey, Seely. You were right about me keeping warm today," he said. "I didn't even get cold coming home."

"You will now," I told him, "if you stand out here talking all night." I smiled to soften my words, and added, "You've got more than a man-sized load of wood already."

That night after supper, Mom washed the dishes, I dried them and put them away. Robert was doing his schoolwork on the kitchen table, while Dad sat quietly smoking his pipe. We were nearly finished with the dishes and I was thinking what a good night it was. We didn't have a lot to feel good about, but Dad had work again and Mom seemed content with her lot.

Dad took a deep draw on his pipe, and through the

cloud of smoke he blew, he said, "Zel, has your daughter told you what she's been up to today?"

Mom's hands got real still in the dishwater and a look of uneasiness crossed her face. "I can't take the full credit for her," Mom answered quietly. "She's your daughter too."

I couldn't think of anything that I'd done wrong, but to make sure of it, I started mentally checking my actions from the time I had gotten out of bed, until right now. I had gotten as far as to when I left the school to go to Avery's store, when I heard Dad's low chuckle.

"Zel, Seely either begged a pair of work gloves from Pete Avery's wife this morning, or she stole them," Dad said. "I'm waiting to hear from Seely which it was. I'd hate to go in there and make a damn fool of myself by offering to pay for a pair of gloves that they hadn't even missed yet."

I didn't know how to tell of the hurt I had felt inside at the sight of Dad working in the almost-zero weather, his hands stiff and purple from the cold. Yet they would expect some kind of explanation for what I had done.

"Well, Seely," Dad said.

I turned full around to face him. "You fixed my shoes good as new," I said, "and I didn't even have to tell you they were done for. You knew it. This morning when I saw that you needed gloves, but you couldn't leave your job to get them, I went to Mrs. Avery and got them for you. I didn't steal them. You owe her thirty-nine cents," I added. "And I promised it on payday."

51

Dad nodded his head. "That's what I figured," he said, quietly.

Mom didn't say anything. She'd had to swallow charity a long while back, and now she was having to face credit, owing someone a debt she'd had no hand in making—but one that she could understand the reason for, I thought.

Dad laid the gloves on the table for Mom to see. The soft yellow fuzz on the palms was worn to the threads by just one day's work.

"I can put leather thumbs and palms on these gloves tonight," Dad said. "And they'll probably last me till nineteen thirty-seven."

Mom snorted good-naturedly. "Rob, that's nearly six weeks away. They'll never last that long, even with patching," she said.

"Nothing lasts forever, Zel," Dad said. "Not even a depression. This work project that I'm on now is the road to something better. You wait and see." He grinned at Mom and added, "We'll find the pot of gold we're looking for at the end of this road."

When Robert and I went to bed, Mom was tracing around the gloves, making a pattern on a piece of leather, and Dad had the awl and darning needle handy, just waiting for her to finish.

chapter six

Roxie wasn't at school the following day, so I didn't find out whether she had met Charlie Buskirk in the furnace room, or not. But when Annabel started down the steps toward the furnace room at noon, Ogretta said she didn't want to eat lunch there. The place gave her the creeps. "The sun's shining, and it wouldn't be too cold in the chimney corner today," Gretta said. "And the wind couldn't hit us there."

It wasn't really a chimney corner. We just called it that because of its shape. The brick wall of the schoolhouse jutted out from the rest of the building at one spot, forming a deep cubby-hole four or five feet wide and making enough room for four people to get out of the wind. If we wanted to, we could sit on the hip-high window ledge that ran all the way around the school-house.

As Gretta, Annabel, and I swung around the corner of the chimney, we saw Russell Williams leaning against the wall in the deep V of the chimney corner, drinking milk from a pint fruit jar. His dinner bucket was sitting open on the window ledge, and it was empty.

"What are you doing here?" Ogretta blurted out in surprise.

Russell wiped the milk from his upper lip. "Drinking my lunch," he said. His lips smiled, but his eyes were dark and sober. "I'll get my bucket and get out of your way."

Russell started to move out of the corner, and Annabel stopped him. "You were here first," she said. "Why don't you ask us to join you? And we'll say, 'Oh, we'd love to.' Then I can divvy up the lunch sacks and we'll all eat together. We're one short today, anyway," she added.

Russell dropped his head and turned away. "I'm no fit company," he said and took his lunch bucket and left.

"I'll be right back," I said, and took off running to catch up with Russell. I knew there had to be something bad wrong with Russell, or something had happened at the Williams place that he couldn't face up to yet. I had seen him after his dad died, and I'd talked to him after Morton Chally had beaten him half to death. But I'd never seen Russell looking as unhappy as he did right now.

Russell stopped walking when I caught his arm, but

54

he didn't look at me. "What is it, Russell?" I said softly, as I stepped in front of him. "What has Chally done to you this time?"

Russell tried to smile and deny his hurt, but his mouth went all crooked and his face crumpled up. He put his hands over his face, then turned quickly and leaned against the brick wall, his shoulders shaking as if they would jar him apart.

I was frightened. I hadn't meant to hurt him more. I only wanted to help, to take away the unhappiness from his eyes and see them smile again. I put my hand on his back, then moved it gently to his shoulder and began to pat him, the way I did Robert sometimes to quiet him.

Finally, his shaking stopped, and Russell took his hands down from his face. But he still kept turned away from me. "I told him that the mare needed a veterinary," Russell said real low. "That she couldn't have the foal without help. But he wouldn't listen. He let my mare die, then he took the foal."

I thought he was finished, but then he said harshly, "He beat the foal's brains out with a single-tree. Said there wasn't enough milk to feed it."

I felt sick at my stomach, like I was going to throw up. "Why, Russell? Why would he do such a thing?"

"He did it out of spite!" Rage and pain made his voice break. "He hates me. He knew that would hurt me worse than anything he could do." He rubbed his face, wiping away all sign of any emotion. When he went on his voice was firm and strong. "I begged him to save my mare," Russell said. "I would've done anything for her.

55

But it didn't do any good," he added quietly. "Then when I was ready to fight him for the colt, Chally knocked me clean across the stable with one lick of his fist. When I woke up, the foal was just as dead as its mother."

I stood there tongue-tied when Russell finished, not able to say a word. To me it was unthinkable that Morton Chally should be allowed to get away with such cruelty.

If Dad knew about what Morton Chally had done, he would see that steps were taken to punish him for it. And Dad would know just what steps to take too. And that's what I finally told Russell, stumbling and falling over the words in my haste to get them said.

"Dad will see to it that Chally never hurts you again," I told him.

Russell shook his head. "Seely, you mustn't tell your dad or anyone else about Morton Chally," he said. "Promise me that you won't."

I hated to do it, but when I saw that he really meant it, I crossed my heart, raised my right hand and promised.

"It would make things worse for me than they are now," he said. "I can stay out of his reach most of the time, but if a fuss is raised, he'll lay in wait to get me."

Russell leaned down and picked up his dinner bucket from where he'd dropped it earlier. "I've caused you to miss your lunch," he said with a small smile.

I gave him back the best smile I could come up with. "I'll go eat now," I said, "and see you later." I started back to the chimney corner.

He waved and walked off, his head held high, and the dinner bucket swinging carelessly at his side.

Annabel and Gretta were munching cheese and crackers and passing a cup of cold potato soup back and forth between them.

"We waited to eat, just like one hog waits for another," Gretta said.

I smiled at her, then looked in the brown bag to see what they had saved for me. "Anyone want half of this peanut butter sandwich?"

"It's all yours," Annabel answered. "And you get all that's left of the potato soup."

I rested my behind on the window ledge and took a bite of the bread and peanut butter. I tried to swallow it, but I couldn't. My throat had closed tight. I put the sandwich back in the bag.

"Seely, you and Russell Williams must be in love," Annabel teased. "You've both lost your appetites, it looks like, and I've heard that's a good sign of it."

Gretta looked at me, then quickly glanced away. "That must be the truth," she said to Annabel. "I've noticed that *you've* hardly touched a bite of food since you met my brother Jay."

Annabel laughed and finished the last of the soup. "I've got to keep up my strength to chase him," she said.

Ogretta slid her bottom off the ledge and came over by me to clear away the lunch things. "Seely, you're as white as a sheet," Gretta said softly. "Don't you feel well?"

57

I shook my head. "Something has upset my stomach," I told her.

Annabel heard my answer to Gretta, and she came over. "I'll bet you and Roxie have got the same thing," she said. "That's why she didn't come to school today. You've both got an acute case of intestinal flu."

Oh Lord, I thought, this must be the week that Annabel is practicing to be a nurse. Every week she changed her mind about what she was going to be when she graduated. She had gone through a phase of being everything from a missionary in China to a movie star. Now it was medicine.

Annabel put her hand on my forehead and wrinkled her own as if in deep thought. "You're sick, all right," she said. "Your face is like ice."

I was saved from the undertaker's parlor by the three minute bell. We ran to the outside toilets, stood in line for a seat, and barely made it into the schoolhouse on time.

Russell and Annabel were already on the school bus, sharing the front seat, when I got there. I sat down behind them, and Peedle Porter moved from a seat farther back into the one next to me.

"I wanted to sit where you do," he said to me.

"Why, Peedle," I teased him. "What will people think?"

"I don't care why they think," he said. "I told my ma that you were the nicest girl in school. You're nice to me on the bus, too," he added.

I didn't know what to say. Peedle Porter was no brighter than he had to be to get by, and sometimes he could aggravate the life out of me. But he said just what he thought, and he never seemed to care whether anyone liked it or not.

Russell Williams turned in his seat to face us. "I tell my mother the same thing, Peedle. She knows that Seely is the best friend I've got in school."

He grinned at me, then winked as I turned red as a cock's comb with embarrassment.

Annabel said, "I'll bet you are coming down with something, Seely. Your face looks like it's on fire now."

Mom said I looked like I was coming down with something when I got home. "I knew you'd get pneumonia walking home through the cold the other night," she said.

I knew I wasn't sick. I just couldn't get the thought of what Morton Chally had done to Russell's mare and colt out of my mind. But I didn't dare tell that to Mom. She'd tell Dad. And I couldn't let him know. Not after I had promised Russell not to breathe a word to him about it.

Friday at school went slowly. The last day of the week always seemed to crawl by or to stand still and not move at all. Roxie wasn't at school again. Her mother sent word that Roxie had a sore throat and a cold. But Annabel said she figured Roxie had stayed home because of something that happened when she met Charlie Buskirk in the furnace room. "If something went wrong and she made a fool of herself, after we warned her not to go," Annabel said "she'd get sick on purpose just so she wouldn't have to face us."

I looked at Gretta, waiting to hear what she had to say about it. But Gretta wouldn't meet my eyes. She fidgeted from one foot to the other and didn't say anything. When I didn't comment one way or the other on why Roxie wasn't in school, Annabel dropped the subject and went on to something else. But for the rest of the day I caught myself thinking of Roxie, instead of my lessons. I was glad when the dismissal bell rang.

When I went to the cloakroom to get my jacket, it was wadded into a ball and lying on the floor in the back corner of the room. I always kept the blue stocking cap that had been Jamie's in my desk in the homeroom. I was afraid it would get lost or stolen if I left it with my jacket. Now I was glad that I had.

I pulled my cap down over my ears and stooped to pick up my jacket. The minute I moved it, the smell of cow manure filled the little room, and I backed away, gagging and choking. I knew what had been done to my jacket, and I had my suspicions about who had done it. Only Elsworth Starnes and Jummy Lewis would be lowdown enough to mess up someone's coat on a day as cold as this one.

I stood and looked at my jacket for a moment, too stunned to think what to do, then I turned and ran down the hall and out to the school bus. I said, "Mr. Avery, will you wait awhile for me? I've lost my coat."

He nodded and motioned for me to be gone.

60

I went directly to the Home Economics room where I knew there would be flour sacks for me to carry my jacket home in and baking soda to put down the odor. I had to empty a bag of flour into a big can to get a sack, but within minutes, I had dumped a box of soda over my jacket and rolled it tight inside the flour sack. I was back to the school bus before Mr. Avery was even ready to leave the schoolyard.

"Didn't find your coat, huh?" he asked.

I ran shivering up the steps and into the bus without answering him.

I went to the very back of the bus, looking for Elsworth Starnes and Jummy Lewis. But I didn't see them. I think I would have dumped the jacket right in their laps if they had been there. I slid my bundle under a seat and sat down where the wind couldn't hit me every time the door was opened.

I turned my back to the rest of the bus and looked out the window. I didn't want to face anyone right then. I was glad when the biggest Knight boy sat down beside me. It would be hard for anyone to see past him and find me hunkered in the seat next to the window.

When there was no one left on the bus but Russell Williams and me, I dragged the bundle from between my feet and went to sit across the aisle from him.

"I didn't see you get on the bus," he said. Then, as if he had just noticed, he said, "Seely, where's your coat? You're going to freeze."

I touched the rolled-up flour sack on the seat beside

me. "My jacket is in here," I said. "Somebody used it today to clean their cow pasture. It's not fit to wear. But I can't throw it away."

Russell started to unbutton his jacket. "Take my coat. I'll be home in a minute. And you've got a long walk after you leave the bus."

I wouldn't take it. I wouldn't see him before Monday, and he'd need it before then. "Besides," I said, "it would just give Chally another reason to pick on you."

"Forget Chally," Russell said. "It's my coat."

I didn't remind him that the mare and foal had been his too, but Chally had used them as an excuse to hurt him.

Russell tried to make me take his coat, right up to the time he was getting off the bus. But I kept on refusing.

"Take your coat and go on home, son," Mr. Avery said. "I figure to turn this bus around in the Robinsons' barnyard tonight. Seely won't have to walk far enough to get cold."

And that is what Mr. Avery did.

I dropped the flour sack that held my soiled jacket onto the back porch and went in the house. I didn't see Mom or Robert as I went through to my bedroom. Once there, I got out of my school clothes and put on the oldest things I could find. Topping them off with an old sweater of Dad's.

I scooped hot coals and ashes out of the firebox in the front room stove and carried the panful outside to build a fire under the washtub. When the water was near to boiling point, I put lye in the water, then I took the flour sack by the corners and dropped my jacket into the tub. I put the sack into the fire and burned it.

Dad came walking across the backyard, home from working on the schoolyard, just as I was dumping the water from the third rinsing of my jacket.

"Seely? Is that you?" Dad said. When I answered, he said, "What in the name of common sense are you doing out here in the dark?"

"Washing cow manure out of my jacket," I answered. "Mom wasn't home, and I wanted to get it done before she got here."

He seemed not to have heard my reason for being outside in the dark. He stopped and waited until I got to him, then we walked together into the house.

"Your mother told me this morning that Aunt Fanny was going to bring Robert home from school today, then they'd go to Oolitic with her. You must have just missed them," Dad added.

I had kept the fires going in both the stoves, and I had supper all ready except for stirring up the cornbread and putting it in the oven. While I did that, Dad strung a line behind the stove and draped my jacket over it to dry. The Red Seal lye had taken a lot of the color out of the jacket, but there was no stain or scent of what had been smeared on it. All it had now was the clean smell of lye, soap, and wood smoke.

I was taking the cornbread out of the oven when we heard Aunt Fanny's car coming into our yard. "Seely, I wouldn't bother your mother with any talk of your jacket," Dad said. "I'll be working at the school again on

Monday, and I'll have a word with Mr. Drayer while I'm there."

Aunt Fanny turned the car around and headed back up the road, and Mom and Robert came into the house. There was no time for any talk about my jacket, even if I had wanted to. And I didn't. Mom had bought sugar and what spices she would need to make pies for Thanksgiving. "Thank goodness, pumpkin pies need only one crust," she said. "Flour and lard are out of reason, they're so costly. But I have plenty of both on hand," she added. "No call to worry about it now."

But I knew she would. The pie crusts would be thin, but they'd be flaky and full to the brim with spicy filling. We had plenty of pumpkin on hand too, which Mom had failed to mention. I wondered what else we would have for Thanksgiving dinner. It was less than a week away, and Dad wouldn't get paid before then.

chapter seven

Soon after school took up on Monday morning, I was called to the principal's office again. Mr. Drayer was the only one in the library when I got there, and he didn't ignore my presence this time or forget I was there.

"Seely," Mr. Drayer began, as soon as he had closed the door behind me, "Pete Avery came to my house last night, and your father left here just minutes ago. They both told me a story about something happening to your jacket here at school Friday. Now, I want you to tell me what you know about this."

"It wasn't a story they told you, Mr. Drayer. It was the truth."

He got red in the face, but he didn't interrupt me.

"When school was out Friday," I went on, "I went to

the cloakroom and found my jacket smeared with cow manure and thrown on the floor. I emptied a sack of flour into a can in the Home Economics room to get something to carry my jacket home in. I couldn't afford to throw it away."

"As I recall," Mr. Drayer said, "it was pretty cold that evening. What did you wear home?"

"I didn't need anything," I said. "Mr. Avery took me all the way home and I didn't have to be out in the weather."

"Seely, do you know who did this?"

"No sir."

"Who do you think did it?"

"Mr. Drayer, could I tell you why I think it, before I say?"

He nodded his head, and said, "Go on."

"Well, Elsworth Starnes has done just about every mean thing he can think of, and nobody does anything about it," I said. "Just last week he tore Peedle Porter's sweater off him, then shoved him down in the bus. Peedle fell against me, and when I helped him to his feet, Elsworth said some nasty things about me because I helped Peedle."

I stopped then to see if Mr. Drayer was still listening to me.

"Go on, Seely," he said. "What happened then?"

This was the part that I dreaded to tell him. But if I didn't, he wouldn't believe that Elsworth Starnes had a reason to mess up my jacket.

"Then I got mad, Mr. Drayer, and I said . . . and I

repeated some gossip that I had heard about his mother. I shouldn't have," I said. "But it was the only way I knew to shut him up. Elsworth raised his hand to strike me, and I hit him in the belly and made him look foolish in front of his friends." I stopped and took a deep breath.

Mr. Drayer made a steeple with his fingers and sat and stared at me over his hands. "Was that the evening you walked home, rather than apologize to Elsworth?"

"Yes, sir."

"And you think that Elsworth is behind this trouble you've had?"

I didn't hesitate a moment. "Yes sir," I said. "I do."

"So do I," Mr. Drayer said. "I've known Elsworth for years, and it's just the sort of thing he'd do to get even."

After saying that I shouldn't have any more trouble with Elsworth once he got through with him, Mr. Drayer asked me if I needed an excuse slip to get into class. I told him that I had study hall the first hour. "Then run along," he said kindly. "And study fast. Your first hour is about up."

As I turned to leave the office I noticed that it was snowing. Not the big, soft, friendly flakes that drift down slow and easy, the kind you can catch in your mouth and play with, but a fine, mean snow that came across the country ninety miles an hour and bit and stung your face when it hit. At the rate this snow was coming, in no time at all it would stack up in the fence corners and cover everything in sight with a blanket of white.

As an excuse to look out the window and see if Dad and the men were working in this snowstorm, I took my pencil to the pencil sharpener and ground it down to a short stub before I finally found Dad's figure bent away from the wind as he wielded the pick and broke ground.

Luck was with me in period two English class. Good luck in one way. I had remembered to bring the newspaper clipping Miss Hendricks had asked for. She had graded the short stories and was passing them out today.

"Before I return these manuscripts to you," Miss Hendricks said, "there is one very unusual story that I would like to have the author read to you."

I was looking at everyone in class, trying to figure out who would be the unlucky one who had to stand in front of the room and read their story. Miss Hendricks was looking at me.

"Seely, do you have the newspaper clipping that gave you the idea for your story?"

"It's here somewhere," I mumbled, and searched through my English book until I found it. I held the little square of newsprint up so she could see that I had it.

"Well, bring it to me," she said.

I took the clipping to Miss Hendricks, then started back to my seat. "Just stay here," she said, touching the edge of her desk with one hand. "I'll want you to read in a minute."

I stood there, embarrassed to the point of death, while Miss Hendricks read the newspaper article to the class. When she had finished, she handed me the story I had turned in as a class assignment. "Now, Seely, you may read your manuscript," she said.

I noticed that it had been graded A— with a red pencil,

68

but other than that the words on the paper were a blur before my eyes.

"What's the matter, Seely?" someone called from the back of the room. "Can't you read your own writing?"

Everyone laughed. Miss Hendricks smiled, and said, "All right, class." Then she nodded at me to go ahead and read.

After the second try, I read, " 'The Hog Calling Contest,' by Seely Robinson," and went on to read the whole story I had written of how a woman from the back hills of Greene County had won the national medal for hog calling. The story ended with one of the judges telling another, "That woman ain't just calling the hogs, she's making love to them in their own tongue."

The class was in an uproar when I finished. Even Miss Hendricks had laughed so hard she was wiping her eyes.

"Thank you, Seely," she said. "That is a fine example of what one can do when the imagination is given a little leeway."

Miss Hendricks gave out the papers then and dismissed the class. Albert Frye stopped in front of me and said, "That's weird. Hogs don't know nothing about love." Miss Hendricks said, "Anything, Albert." I didn't say anything. I looked at my feet until he went away.

At lunch, Annabel looked at me kind of funny, and said, "I used to think you were quiet and backward because your head was empty. But now I think it's because your head is so full of stuff that your mouth doesn't know what to let loose on us."

We were sitting on the top row of bleachers in the

gymnasium today. Gretta had refused to eat in the furnace room ever again, and it was too cold and snowy to go outside. The boys were practicing basketball, and there were a lot of other kids there eating their lunch and watching the game.

Roxie grinned at me and said, "Annabel, do you reckon everyone who sees us with her will think we're as odd as she is, or will they just assume we're a bunch of brains?"

Ogretta put her arm around me and scooted closer on the bench. "Don't pay any attention to them, Seely. In their stupid way, they are trying to tell you how proud they are that Miss Hendricks picked your story above all the rest."

I looked at Annabel, Roxie, and Ogretta. My three friends. And they looked back at me. "Don't be such an old sobersides," Annabel said. "Smile, you little idiot. You're our hero!" Then they all three hugged me and laughed.

"What's all the commotion?" someone on the next bench asked. And Albert Frye answered, "It's that nutty Seely Robinson and her friends. They're apt to do anything."

That broke us up again. We laughed so hard and so loud that they got up and moved to another spot.

After a while, Annabel said, "Seely, have you been making up stories and writing them down for a long time?"

"Not very long," I answered. "I used to write everything that happened around our house in a notebook.

70

But then the notebooks got filled up and there was nothing happening to write about anyhow. So I started making up stories about imaginary people. All kinds of things can happen to people when they are just characters in a story. But it's not as though they were really alive," I added.

"But why do you do it?" she persisted.

I couldn't tell her that I felt like I had to write these things. That it was like a craving for candy. I had to have pencil and paper handy or I felt lost. I smiled at Annabel and said, "I'm too old to play with dolls. And I'm too young to date boys. So I write stories to pass the time."

"Believe me, Seely," Annabel said. "Boys are a lot more fun than writing. That's hard work!"

Roxie snorted. That's the only word for the sound she made. "You don't know what work is until you've fought off Charlie Buskirk for an hour," she said. "That man is an animal and I hate him! I wish I didn't have to see him every day on the school bus."

Roxie hadn't mentioned being sick when she came back to school today. It was as if she hadn't been absent. This was the first she had said about her meeting with Charlie Buskirk, and from the sound of her voice I didn't think we'd have to worry about Roxie and the bus driver any more.

"Roxie, I told you that what you felt for Charlie was animal magnetism," Annabel said. "The next time you get that feeling, visit the zoo and get it out of your system."

Gretta and I smiled. We didn't take Roxie's outburst

71

any more seriously than Annabel did. Neither one of us went out with boys or wanted to. We both thought one good book was worth ten boys. Unless two of them were Byron Tyson and Russell Williams. And they weren't the beau type boys. They were friends.

The school bus was cold that evening, and the aisle between the two rows of seats was a wet, sloppy path from the snow that was tracked in on our shoes. I had to sit about halfway back in the bus, but Peedle Porter found his way back to sit beside me. This was one day, I thought, that I could do without Peedle's company.

He had no more than sat down when he whispered to me, "Did you hear what happened to Elsworth Starnes?"

I said, "No, I didn't, Peedle. What happened to Elsworth?"

"He got put on probation. Do you know what that means?"

"It means he has to behave himself from now on," I said.

"That's not all it means," Peedle said. "It means that his ma or pa has to bring him to school every day, just like a first-grader, and pick him up after school. You don't see him on the bus, do you?"

I had to admit that I didn't see Elsworth Starnes anywhere on the bus. "And you won't either," Peedle assured me. "He won't cause you any more trouble."

He sat back in his seat as if he had been personally responsible for getting rid of Elsworth and making this bus safe for me to ride home on. I looked at the proud set of his thin shoulders and the pleased look on his face, and I was ashamed of myself. It wasn't his fault that he'd been born the way he was.

"Thanks for telling me about Elsworth Starnes, Peedle. I appreciate it."

"I was glad to do it," Peedle replied, happily.

When Mr. Avery stopped the school bus to let me off at the end of our road, he said, "If I'm not here by broad daylight in the morning, you'll know that I'm not coming. The way this snow is coming down, we may be snowed in by morning." He started to close the bus door, then opened it again. "Seely, don't stand out there waiting for me in the cold," he said. "If I'm coming, I'll blow my horn to give you plenty of time to get here."

The road to our house was covered smooth with snow, and I couldn't tell where the level ground left off and the ruts and holes began. I stumbled into the ruts, and fell into the holes. By the time I got home, I was wet with snow up to my waist.

Robert had gotten home not too long before me. The overalls and shirt that he'd worn to school were steaming as they dried on the line behind the stove. His wet shoes were dripping into the woodbox.

The minute I stepped through the door, Mom said, "Get over here by the stove and shed those wet clothes." I didn't have to be told twice to get close to the fire. I was chilled through and through. I brushed the snow from my head and shoulders and it spit and sizzled as it hit the hot stove.

Dad wasn't home yet. The hook on the door was

empty of his coat and cap, and the woodbox was nearly down to the last stick of wood.

"As soon as I get warm," I told Mom, "I'll bring in some stove wood. I can change into dry clothes later." When she started to object, I said, "There's no sense in getting my clothes wet twice in one night."

There was a pile of freshly split logs with hardly any snow on it yet. I figured that Mom must have been cutting wood and stopped when Robert got home from school. I filled my arms with the driest wood I could find, then added a few more logs for good measure and carried them to the porch. I made three trips from the woodpile to the porch before my hands got so cold that I couldn't feel the splinters. But when I got it all inside, we had enough wood in the house to last us through the night.

Dad got home soon after. I went to the bedroom and put on my flannel nightgown and an old flannel shirt of Dad's that I used as a robe and went to the kitchen for supper. Dad said the work foreman had taken them off the schoolyard and into Oolitic to shovel snow from the streets. They had been shoveling snow all evening, and if there wasn't a letup of the blizzard before long, they'd be shoveling snow until Thanksgiving.

The snow stopped sometime during the night, and a thin crust froze over the top of it. But from all appearances, the snow was over for a while. When I left the house to catch the school bus, it was cold and clear as crystal. There were even a few stars still showing in the sky.

74

I was nearing the top of the ridge when I heard the horn. True to his word, Mr. Avery was laying on his horn, letting me know that he was at the end of the road, and he'd wait for me.

Even though it wasn't as cold as the day before, Mr. Avery had warmed up the bus while he waited for me. I wasn't late. He had come early on purpose.

That evening after school, Russell Williams sat down beside me on the bus, and Annabel Grewe and Peedle Porter took the seat directly behind us. Riding the school bus, I thought, was just like sitting down at the supper table, everyone had their place and they sat there almost always.

Peedle leaned forward and shook Russell's shoulder to get his attention. "Russell," he said, "would you go rabbit hunting with me this evening? We could track them easy in the snow."

Russell turned in his seat and smiled at Peedle. "I'd like to," he said, "but it will be pitch dark before I get the milking done."

He started to face forward again, then turned back to Peedle. "Uncle Lester, my mother's brother, is coming to our place early in the morning to go hunting for our four-legged turkeys, Peedle. If we get more rabbits than we can use, I'll bring a couple over for your ma."

Peedle's smile covered his face. "Ma would be much obliged," he told Russell. "She's partial to good rabbit stew."

Russell and Peedle talked hunting and the best way to

cook what they caught, until the bus stopped at Peedle's lane. Everyone left the bus at that stop except Russell and me, Peedle taking the dirt track up the hollow and Annabel and the Knight boys going over the hill in the other direction.

"I'm glad that you're the last one left on the bus with me," I told Russell.

He smiled and cuffed my arm lightly. "Me too," he said.

By this time, the bus was coming up to the crossroad that formed one corner of the Williams place. Russell got his dinner bucket from between his feet, gathered up his books, and stood up, ready to get off the bus as soon as it stopped.

Mr. Avery opened the bus door. Russell said, "I'll see you Monday," and stepped off the bus.

I watched as he cut across the field, making long tracks in the snow, as he headed toward home.

When I left the school bus, I crossed the road to the mailbox, hoping to find a letter from Julie saying that she would be home for Thanksgiving. But like every other day, when I checked the box, it was empty.

chapter eight

Wednesday was our last
day of school until the next Monday. We had Thursday
and Friday off for Thanksgiving. The wind had blown
the snow thin, but Dad said he thought there was still
enough snow on the ground to track a rabbit or two for
our Thanksgiving dinner.

Mom had asked Nellie and Mr. Paully to have dinner
with us. She had asked Gus Tyson and Aunt Fanny too,
but they were driving to Salem to spend a few days with
Grandpa Winslow. Byron would come there from Vincennes to meet them, Gus said. And they wouldn't start
back to Jubilee until Byron left on Sunday to go back
to college. I thought it was just as well that they couldn't
make it to our house for dinner. Mom was getting fidgety
and fussy just fixing for the preacher and Nellie.

The house smelled of spices and good hot food when I got home from school Wednesday night. Four pumpkin pies were still steaming from the oven, and Mom yelled at me to not slam the door. "There's a hickory-nut cake in the oven," she said. "And I don't want it to fall."

I closed the door gently, and even before I took off my coat and cap, I asked, "When are we going to eat supper? I'm starved."

"As soon as your daddy gets home," Mom answered. Then in the same breath, "Seely, don't take off your wraps until you've brought in a few sticks of stove wood."

I stopped unbuttoning my jacket and began to button it back up to my chin. Mom tiptoed to the stove and opened the oven door as gently as taking eggs from a brooding hen, checked the rising cake, then closed the oven quiet as a breath.

"Take care that you don't throw the wood into the woodbox and jar the whole house," she cautioned me, and shooed me out the door.

It would have been too dark to see the woodpile but for the snow. It was white all around, except for the dark spot where the wood had been split and stacked in a high cone. I carried two armloads to the porch and piled it near the kitchen door, then I went back for a third load, which I carried into the kitchen to start filling the woodbox.

I'd made two trips to the porch for wood before Mom noticed. "Lands sake, Seely, stop swinging that door open," she said. "The house is getting to be as cold as a barn."

I closed the door, took off my jacket and stocking cap, and went to my room to hang them up. As I went through the front room, Robert was on his knees in front of the walnut stand table, rubbing and wiping at it with a rag soaked in cedar oil. The whole room smelled of it.

"Don't touch nothing," he ordered. "And don't leave nothing lying around. We've got to keep this room looking neat for them tomorrow," he whispered with a look over his shoulder toward the kitchen.

I hunkered down so my eyes would be on a level with his. "Nellie Fender has been in this house a million times," I said. "She won't mind a speck of dust here and there."

"It's not Nellie that Mom's worried about," Robert answered indignantly. "It's Mr. Paully. I guess preachers are not like other people." His face was puzzled. "They never get their house messed-up like we do, and they just eat special dinners that take a lot of fussing with."

I smiled at him and tried to tousle his hair, but he jerked his head away. I stood up and started on toward the room we shared. "Everything looks fine, Robert. Even fine enough for a preacher," I told him. "Leave it now, and get washed for supper. We'll be eating in a few minutes."

I should have told Robert the difference between nothing and anything, I thought. Julie had read me the riot act when she had heard me do the same thing once. "Nothing is a void," Julie had said firmly. "You can't see it, or touch it, and you can't hold it in your hand. It's nonexistent, therefore it's impossible to have nothing. So don't say that we've got nothing," she added in a superior way. "It shows your ignorance."

I wondered where Julie was right now, and where she would eat her Thanksgiving dinner. I knew that she would be in all our hearts and minds as we sat down at the table tomorrow.

Dad got four rabbits. After they were dressed and hung from a porch rafter to freeze overnight, we ate supper. Beans and cornbread. I hoped that Mom would bring one of the pumpkin pies to the table and cut it. But she didn't offer to, and I didn't want to be the one to ask for it.

Nellie and Mr. Paully came over early on Thanksgiving Day. Nellie had brought a kettle of Irish potatoes, which she set on the stove to cook, and the milk and butter that would be needed later for mashing them. She put them in the windowbox to keep cool.

Dad didn't usually cotton to preachers, but he and the Reverend Mr. Paully got along like a couple of old coon hunters. Dad loaded his pipe and offered the tobacco pouch to the preacher. Mr. Paully refused the tobacco. He said, "I don't use it, but I do like the smell of a good pipe or wood smoke on a cold day."

Dad smiled then and said why didn't they get out from under their women's feet and go outside where he could enjoy them both to his heart's content. They went to get their coats, and Dad pulled his old cap down over his ears. Dad was tall, but the preacher was taller. And a lot thinner too. He didn't wear a cap when they left the house, but went bareheaded into the cold and let his long black hair blow in the wind. Robert went out after them.

Mom and Nellie looked out the window after the men, then they smiled at each other. "A man can be a bit of a trial at times," Nellie said hesitantly. "But Lord, what a comfort he is to have around the rest of the time."

Mom laughed and agreed with Nellie. Then she touched Nellie's bright red hair. "You make a fine-looking couple," she said. "You kind of balance each other in color and temperament."

I was setting the table, trying to match the knives and forks and spoons at each place. Mom said that it didn't matter that they weren't all alike, just that each person got the same pattern.

Mom had been up half the night, it seemed like to me, ironing the white linen tablecloth and napkins to match. She had complained this morning when we put it on the table, that it had lain in the trunk for so long it had turned yellow. She couldn't bring the whiteness completely back, she said.

But it looked fine to me. And I knew Nellie and Mr. Paully would think it was really grand. If they even so much as noticed it beneath the load of food that was being prepared to put on the table.

81

Mom had the baked rabbit basting in brown gravy in the big iron roaster. Green beans that had been canned last sumer were simmering on the back of the stove, seasoned with a chunk of bacon. And Nellie's potatoes, which would be the last thing to fix, were nearly ready to mash and whip into a mouth-watering delight.

"Seely, stop your dilly-dallying," Mom said, "and put these sweet pickles in Grandmother Curry's crystal dish."

I took the jar of pickles out of Mom's hand and went to the cupboard to get Grandma's dish. We only used her dishes on very special occasions. Mom was afraid that one of us kids would break Grandmother Curry's dishes. "And they can't be replaced," she always said, after cautioning us to handle them carefully.

I couldn't have been more careful if the crystal dish had been a nestful of delicate blue robin eggs.

When the table was laden with food, and there wasn't another thing to do, Mom stepped to the kitchen door and called Dad. Robert answered her call, and a few minutes later, we heard two men and a boy stamping the snow off their feet on the back porch.

Robert was the first one through the door. "Whew, it's cold," he said, and shivered as he rubbed his hands together.

"Wash your hands, so you can eat dinner," Mom told him.

Dad and Mr. Paully entered the room right on Robert's heels.

"We've got to wash our hands before we can eat,"

Robert told Mr. Paully. Mom flushed to the roots of her hair.

Nellie smiled, then covered her mouth with her hand so that Mom wouldn't see it.

There were six at our table again. The same as there had been in our family before we had lost Jamie to the flood waters and Julie had gone away to live. But today, good neighbors sat in their places. Mr. Paully bowed his head to say grace, and I closed my eyes. After a moment, I opened them again to look at the ones who were around our table today.

"Dear heavenly Father," Mr. Paully began. "Thank you for this food which You have seen fit to provide . . ." I was looking at Mom and remembering the night she had thanked God for a few puny potatoes on our table. ". . . Bless these friends in Your presence at this table, and the loved ones who can't be with us here today." Suddenly, Mr. Paully raised his head and his dark eyes met mine, my eyes wide open and wet with tears for the ones who would never be with us again. I lowered my eyes, but not before I saw the compassion and understanding in his soft, dark ones. "Comfort those who sorrow for them," Mr. Paully went on, "and bring joy to their hearts. Amen."

His eyes went first to his wife, Nellie, who was no doubt thinking of her boys and wanting them near even though she knew they were better off in that place for the criminally insane. She smiled and brushed at her eyes as Mr. Paully turned to Dad and said, " I never saw a finer spread of food than Sister Robinson has laid before us here today."

Dad disliked hearing Mom called sister by the preacher, but you'd never have known it from the way he answered Mr. Paully.

"Then let's not allow it to get cold," Dad said. "Help yourself to what you can reach, and ask for what you can't lay hand to."

"Take a biscuit, Seely," he said, "and pass them on around the table."

Robert was sitting next to me. I put a biscuit on his plate, took one for myself, then passed the plate to Mom. She was sitting at one end of the table and Dad at the other. Nellie and Mr. Paully sat side by side, Nellie on Mom's right, and Mr. Paully to Dad's left.

I noticed that Robert couldn't take his eyes off the preacher. He seemed mesmerized by him. And I could see why. Mr. Paully's black eyes flashed as he talked. Now and then his eyes would come to rest on Nellie, or Robert and me, as he told of other days in other places, long before he ever came to Greene County.

Dad nodded his head and spoke whenever an answer seemed to be expected of him. But mostly, he sat and listened as attentively as Robert, and never once interrupted Mr. Paully.

It was nearly dark when the Reverend Mr. Paully took Nellie by the hand and said they had to be going. Mom kissed Nellie, shook the preacher's hand, and Dad walked them to the gate and waved them on their way.

"The Lord surely got Himself a talker when He

enlisted the help of Mr. Paully," Dad said, when he came back to the house. "My ears are still ringing from the sound of his voice." He chuckled.

Mom smiled. "It's been a good day," she said. "I've hardly had time to think, much less miss—" She paused, and turned her face away. "Mr. Paully brought the feeling of Thanksgiving into this house," Mom began again. "The last year or so, it didn't seem like I had anything to be thankful for. But he made me see that it wasn't just what we had today that we owed thanks for, but all we'd been allowed to have and know up to now. He talked a good bit," she added, "but he made sense."

"That he did," Dad replied quietly. "That he did!"

chapter nine

Dad worked on the Friday after Thanksgiving. He came home long after dark, his feet wet and overalls mud-caked to his knees. They had been cleaning out culverts and drain ditches, he told Mom. "A damn foolish bit of work," he said, getting out of his muddy clothes. "They'll be clogged up and useless again before the February thaws."

He took a slip of paper from the bib pocket of his overalls and handed it to Mom. "My first week's pay," he said. "Twelve dollars and fifty cents. I'll sign it, and the first time Aunt Fanny goes to Oolitic you can go with her and lay in supplies."

I cleared the table after supper and did the dishes, while Mom sat at the table with Dad and made a list of the things she hoped to buy with Dad's paycheck. I had promised to play numbers with Robert as soon as I was finished with the dishes, and he'd gone to the front room to lay out the cards. I dried the last dish, hung the towel over the line to dry, and started out of the room.

Dad said, "Seely, didn't you go to school with the Williams boy?"

I said, "Russell? Yes, we're both in the tenth grade." I stopped and waited to find out why he had asked about Russell.

"Emil Porter lives just up the hollow from the Williams place," Dad said. "And he was telling me that they'd had a bad hunting accident over there yesterday."

"I hope Morton Chally shot himself," I said. "He's the meanest man I ever heard tell of."

"No," Dad said. "It was the boy."

I just stood there with my mouth open, waiting for Dad to go on. To tell the rest of it.

"Any grown man ought to have more sense than to try to climb a fence with a loaded gun," Dad said. "But Emil says that's what happened. Chally lost his balance and his hold on the shotgun as he went over the fence. When he grabbed for the gun, it went off and struck the boy in the back."

"That Morton Chally did it on purpose." I said. "Russell will tell you, Chally would do anything to hurt him." I was angry to think that Chally had been able to hurt Russell again and spoke louder than need be for Dad to hear me.

"The boy can't say one way or another, Seely," Dad said gently. "He never knew what hit him."

87

I couldn't believe it. I wouldn't believe it. "Russell?" I said. "You mean, he killed him?" Dad nodded his head, then began to fill his pipe. A sign that the talking was done with. But I wasn't through talking. There was more to be said about Morton Chally, and I was going to say it . . . come what may.

"Chally has beaten Russell ever since he moved into that house," I said. "He killed Russell's mare and newborn colt, and now he has deliberately killed Russell. He's the one that ought to be shot," I added, my face wet with angry tears.

Dad got his pipe going and took a couple of deep draws on it. "I don't want to hear talk like that in this house," he said. "It was an accident."

"That's what Morton Chally wants people to think," I said angrily.

Dad frowned at me. "I won't tell you again, Seely," he said. "That kind of talk will only cause trouble."

"I'd like to cause Morton Chally trouble," I answered, too hurt to care if Dad slapped me for sassing him. "He got away with the other things he did to Russell. He shouldn't be allowed to get away with this too."

"If he is guilty of murdering that boy, he'll pay for it," Dad said quietly. "But that's not for you to say, Seely. Talking about it will just get you in trouble," he added. "Not the Chally man."

Robert called me then to come and play cards. He was waiting for me. I realized that I had heard him call my name before, but I hadn't paid any attention to it. "Go on, Seely," Dad said. "Play with the boy."

88

I played numbers with Robert, and he beat me at every game. Finally, he gave up in disgust and went to bed. "You're no fun tonight," he grumbled.

I was so filled with indignation toward Morton Chally and so shocked that Russell was gone forever that I would have been poor company for the devil himself this night.

Dad went to work the next morning, even though it was Saturday, and not much later in the day Aunt Fanny came by to see if Mom wanted to go to Oolitic with her. Mom said she did and went to get her coat and hat.

"I want to get back early," Aunt Fanny said, as Mom came into the kitchen, all ready to go. "The Williams boy's funeral is this afternoon and I want to pay my respects. Would you like to go with me?" she asked Mom.

Mom said she thought not. "It wouldn't be seemly," she said. "I don't know the family. Never met the boy's mother."

"Seely, you knew Russell Williams." Aunt Fanny turned to me. "Wouldn't you like to go?"

"No, she wouldn't," Mom answered for me, shortly and to the point. "And if we're going to get to Oolitic and back today, we'd better get started." She opened the door, and Aunt Fanny followed her outside.

Russell Williams' name wasn't mentioned at our house again. I know Mom and Dad must have thought of him, the same as I did, but we didn't talk about what had happened to him or speculate on the circumstances surrounding his death. I guess they felt as helpless as I did when it came to doing anything about it.

Pete Avery was awfully quiet when I got on the school bus on Monday morning. Usually, I was the quiet one who didn't want to talk. Mr. Avery would joke and jolly me out of it. I'd be wide awake and ready to face the day by the time we got to the Williams place. But this morning, Mr. Avery seemed to grow even more quiet as we went by the stop at the crossroads, and he speeded on down the road to the next stop.

I sat, as I always did, in the seat directly behind Mr. Avery. He raised his head, and his eyes met mine in the wide rearview mirror, then he quickly looked away.

"Seely, do you know about what happened to Russell?" He kept his head down, and his eyes on the road ahead.

"Yes," I answered. "But I'm not supposed to talk about it."

Mr. Avery didn't say any more, and pretty soon he started slowing down for the next stop.

Peedle Porter slipped quietly into the seat beside me, and Annabel took the seat behind us. The Knight boys went on toward the rear of the bus.

"Wasn't that awful about Russell?" Annabel couldn't wait for the bus to begin moving before she started talking. "I went to the funeral," she said. "Hardly any of the kids were there and not one bunch of flowers. The Challys didn't want flowers, they said. I guess they didn't want the kids he went to school with to be there either," Annabel added. "If they had, they'd have waited till today to have his funeral."

I knew what she meant by this. Last year when Carlie Wilson died of pneumonia, school had been let out for the day and the kids taken to the church by school buses to attend his funeral.

I turned my face to the window and didn't answer Annabel. After the next stop, I heard her telling it all over again to whoever had sat down in the seat beside her.

I felt crowded in my seat and moved nearer to the window to give Peedle more room. A moment later, I was just as crowded as before. I turned to tell Peedle to scoot over; he didn't need my seat and his too. But when I looked at him, I couldn't say a word.

Peedle was sitting stiff in his seat, his eyes straight ahead. As I watched, tears formed in round blobs on his lashes, then slid slowly down his cheek. I found his hand on the seat between us and put my hand over his. I didn't care who saw me holding Peedle's hand, nor what they had to say about it. I'd found one person who cared as much as I did that Russell was gone, and I meant to give any comfort I could to him.

I turned back to the window, and after a moment, I felt his fingers close around my hand and hold on tight. We rode all the way to school like that, with neither one of us saying a word. And if anyone noticed, they didn't say anything either.

The school was a-buzz that day, and for most of the

91

week, with talk about Russell Williams and what the kids called his "stupid accident." They said it had to be stupidity or a lack of common sense that Morton Chally had shown, to be handling a loaded gun so carelessly. The general feeling was that the accident had been the result of Chally's stupidness.

I didn't talk to anyone about it. But I couldn't help hearing some of the things that were being said. By the end of the week, instead of saying "Get Lost," to someone they didn't want around, they said, "Send him out to hunt rabbits with Morton Chally." And they'd laugh. I felt like I was the only one who remembered Russell as a person warm and full of life, wanting only to grow up.

I seemed to have inherited Peedle Porter for a seatmate on the school bus—going to school and coming home. But I didn't mind Peedle's company. He was quiet most of the time. Hardly saying a word except, "Good morning," when he got on the bus, and then, "See you tomorrow," when he got off at his lane in the afternoon. But this Friday, Peedle seemed fidgety, like he wanted to say something, but he wasn't sure how I would take it.

Finally, he said, "Seely, I still feel bad that my friend Russell got killed. Don't you think I ought to feel better by now?"

I said, "Don't think about him, Peedle. And after a while you won't feel so bad."

"I'll try," he said. "But every day, when I don't see him, I get sorrier and sorrier."

92

I tried to tell Peedle what Mr. Paully had said on Thanksgiving Day about being glad for the time and the joy we'd had in another's friendship and not sorrow for what we couldn't have. But I don't think I did a very good job of convincing Peedle. He said, "Seely, can you be so glad you knew someone that you don't feel sorry when they're gone?"

I said, "I don't know, Peedle."

I thought about his question long after he had left the bus, and I tried to remember Mr. Paully's exact words, thinking that I might find the answer there. But they were all mixed up with being thankful for what we had, comforting the ones who sorrowed, and keeping joy in our heart. I'd done what I could about comforting Peedle, I thought. But there wasn't any joy in my heart to speak of.

chapter ten

The snow we got the week of Thanksgiving was just a warning of what was to come. On the first of December a blizzard came swooping down the hollows, covering the roads and drifting even with the fence posts on either side of the road. Dad bought overshoes on credit at Averys' store for Robert and me to wear to school, then wrapped gunny sacks over his own shoes and up to his knees to wear to work. WPA boots, he called them. Work Proof Arctics. And made a joke of having to dry them out over the stove every night.

My birthday came during the first week of December. I was fifteen years old. But I couldn't see any difference in me than when I was twelve. A little taller, maybe. But still as straight up and down as a broomstick. Dad

94

hadn't cut my hair for a long while now, and it hung to below my shoulders and turned under on the ends of its own accord. Where once it had been the color of skimmed milk, it had darkened until it was the same honey color as Robert's hair. I had given up all hopes of ever being dark-headed like Mom and Julie and having a natural curl.

As the days went by and the time for our break from school drew nearer, all anyone could talk about was Christmas. What they were giving and all they hoped to receive in return. I told Annabel Grewe that I didn't expect we'd have much of a Christmas. But I was wrong. Julie came home from college, and we had an early Christmas.

When I got on the bus after school on Friday, the last day of school before Christmas and the beginning of our break, she was sitting in the seat directly behind Mr. Avery looking at every face that came through the bus door. I came up the steps, and her face lit up with a wide smile. I just stood and looked at her. It didn't seem possible that this neat, smartly dressed woman could be my sister Julie.

Still smiling, Julie patted the empty seat beside her. "Sit down, Seely. You're holding up traffic."

Same as always, I minded her. "How did you get here?" I asked. "Why didn't you let us know you were coming?"

"I didn't know it myself until yesterday," Julie replied. "One of the girls at school was hitchhiking home to Bedford for the holidays, and she asked me to come with her. But don't tell Mom that I hitchhiked," she added. "I'm going to say I came with a girl who lives in Bedford, and let it go at that."

Everyone looked at Julie as they got on the bus and when they left it. But no one said anything about Mr. Avery's rule that only regular students were allowed to ride on this bus. I suppose they could've thought that Julie was a new teacher who would be starting at the school after vacation. She looked important enough to be a teacher.

When we got to the end of our road, Mr. Avery lifted Julie's suitcase off the bus, then offered his hand to help her down the steps. I was down the steps in two leaps. To Julie's thanks for the ride home, Mr. Avery said, "Glad to do it, Miss. I know how pleased your folks will be to see you."

I wanted to carry her suitcase for her, but Julie wouldn't let me. "There's really nothing in it," she said.

"Then you're carrying a bag full of non-existent substance," I said with a smile, reminding her of the time she had tried to break me of the habit of saying "nothing" when I meant "anything."

Julie laughed. "Oh, Seely. Don't you ever forget anything?"

I ran up the road a ways, talking to her over my shoulder, then I waited for Julie to nearly catch up before I ran a little farther. I kept warmer that way, and she was never close enough to see that I was shivering and shaking from the cold.

We were over the ridge and going down the other

side when Julie stopped to look at our house, sitting half-way to the foot of the hill.

"I'd forgotten that it was so far from the main road," she said. Then, "Seely, how do you stand it back here, away from everyone and everything?"

"I like it," I said. I didn't even have to stop and wonder why. I knew. "Julie, I like this part of the country, and I like the people who live around here," I added quietly.

She moved her head slowly from side to side, as if she couldn't ever understand how anyone could possibly want to live in a place like this. Julie stood there a moment longer, then followed me on down the hill toward the house.

Mom was so happy to see Julie that she didn't even think to ask her how she got here. She wiped her eyes on her apron tail, and said, "Honey, had I known that you were coming home, I would've fixed you a good supper."

Julie said, "Ah, Mom. Whatever you've got ready will be fine for me."

She gave Mom a quick hug, then knelt and reached her arms out to Robert who stood watching shyly from the door to the front room. "Come here, and give your big sister a hug," she said softly.

Robert's shy smile spread until it covered his face. "Aw, you're not so very big," he said. And to prove it her nearly bowled her over with his exuberant embrace. They romped and tusseled a moment, mostly Julie trying to hug Robert, and he pretending he didn't want her to, until Mom called a halt to their rowdy play. "There'll be time enough for that later," she told Robert.

Julie was still wearing her hat and coat. She took them off now and stood holding them, like company who didn't know where to put their things.

"Julie, when do you have to go back up there?" Mom asked.

She never said school in relation to Julie. Not if she could help it. It was as though Mom thought there was something disgraceful about a nineteen-year-old girl still being in school.

"I'll have to leave day after tomorrow," Julie replied. "I have to be at work on Monday."

"But that's Christmas Eve."

Julie just smiled. I beckoned to her, and she followed me to the bedroom that I shared with Robert. I took Julie's things off her hands and hung her coat on a hook next to mine in the closet and put her hat on the shelf above it. Before I closed the closet door, I ran my hands over the soft wool of the coat and the silk lining. Once again, I felt like Julie was a stranger. She looked like my sister, but I didn't know her any more.

"Lord, it's cold in here." Julie sat on the edge of my bed and wrapped her arms around herself to stop her shivering. "Does Dad still persist in keeping the bedroom door closed to save heat?"

She smiled at me and I smiled back, and nodded my head. "We never open the door to the upstairs," I said. "I doubt that anyone has even been in those rooms since Mom covered the windows with old newspapers to keep out the cold."

98

"Then I guess you have to share your bed with me tonight. Just like old times," she said.

"I don't mind, if you don't," I said. "Like Robert said, you're not so very big. You won't take up much room at all."

There was the sound of feet scuffing the snow, then the door opened and closed. Julie said, "Dad's home." She jumped to her feet and ran out of the room.

Dad was holding his hands over the stove to warm them when we entered the kitchen. He turned toward us, his hands still outstretched, and said, "Well, Sis." Julie walked into his open arms, and he stood there patting her back and smiling.

"It's good to have you home, Sis," Dad said, when Julie finally stepped away. And I thought to myself, that's the first time I have ever seen Dad hug one of us kids.

After supper, Julie opened her suitcase and brought out the gifts she had carried to us from Terre Haute. A five-pound ham for Mom and Dad, a bone-handled pocket knife for Robert, and a slim, silver-colored pen and pencil set for me. "And these will work," Julie said with a laugh, as I took them from her hand.

The only other pen and Eversharp pencil I had ever owned had been a gift from a boy in the sixth grade. And they had been worn out and broken before he ever gave them to me.

"Julie, I can use these forever," I said, already scribbling my name on a piece of paper. "Look how fine they

99

write." I held the paper for Julie to see. "I'll keep them forever and I'll never need any others," I said.

"Seely, it's just a dime store set," Julie said. "They're not made to last any time." She said this almost as if she was apologizing for giving them to me. Then she turned away to watch Dad open the blades on Robert's knife for him.

"He's not too young for a knife like that, is he?" Julie asked Dad.

Dad shook his head no, not taking his eyes off the knife in his hands. "Come spring," he said, "Robert will have the best alder whistles in the county. And with this," he added, holding out the knife, "he can make his own this year."

While the rest of us had been exclaiming over our gifts and admiring them, Mom had stood quietly at the table, her hand resting on the five-pound ham.

"Julie, we didn't know you'd be here," Mom said, her voice filled with misery. "So we don't have a thing to give you."

Julie moved to face Mom across the table. "Mom, just to be here with you all is my gift," she said softly. "That's the only thing I wanted for Christmas. But I couldn't come here empty-handed, getting so much and not giving anything in return. You taught me that," Julie added with a smile.

Julie slept with me that night. Once, when she had first left home, I'd thought that I would never get used to the empty space she had left in our bed. Now, I wondered how it would feel to have her beside me. She didn't seem like the same person that I used to share my bed with.

I slid to the far side of the bed and left most of it for Julie. Lying stiff and straight, I went to sleep not touching her. But when I woke up the next morning, we were curled together in the middle of the bed. Julie was snuggled to my back with her arm resting around my waist, just the same way we had slept as children.

We had our Christmas dinner that day. Mom and Julie worked together preparing the food, and I kept the woodbox and water bucket filled for them. Dad told Robert to put on his boots and bundle up good. "This is no place for a couple of men," he said.

Dad wrapped his feet in his WPA boots, and said to Mom, "We'll walk to Jubilee and talk to Gus Tyson." She nodded her head as if this was something they had discussed earlier, and she agreed that he should. A few minutes later Dad and Robert left the house.

The kitchen never seemed warmer or friendlier than it did that day. Mom and Julie laughed as they bumped into each other going back and forth to the stove with their hands full. They didn't even complain when I got in their way. My job was to keep the mixing dishes washed up, so they could be used over again, and the clutter cleared away. They could dirty dishes and clutter the kitchen faster than I could wash and clear space for them.

I set the table with Mom's good dishes, using Grandma Curry's long-stemmed fruit bowl, filled with canned spiced peaches, as a centerpiece. By the time Dad and

Robert got home from Jubilee, dinner was ready to put on the table, and the kitchen looked as if it had never been used. Everything was shining clean and nothing was out of place.

"Now, the Reverend Mr. Paully would be bound to say grace over a meal like this," Dad said, when we were all at the table. "But I reckon the Lord knows without being told how we feel here today."

He sliced the ham and put a generous piece on each plate as it was passed to him. We helped ourselves to the beans and potatoes and rice pudding that was on the table.

"Gus says that Byron won't be coming home for Christmas," Dad said. "He has part-time work, clerking in a clothing store in Vincennes, and Byron's afraid he'd lose his job if he took time off to come home."

I looked at Julie sitting across the table from me. Half a wish come true was more than I had expected. I had wished that both Byron and Julie would be home for Christmas, but as long as only half of the wish got answered, I was glad it was Julie's half.

"I talked to Gus about driving you back to Terre Haute," Dad said, his eyes on Julie. "I figured that could be our Christmas present to you," he finished, his voice husky.

Dad cleared his throat, then went on. "Gus said that him and Aunt Fanny would be at the end of our road about daylight in the morning to get you. By leaving early, Gus figures they can be back home here before dark tomorrow night."

I never knew when Julie got up and got dressed and left the house the next morning. When I woke at first light, and hurried out to the kitchen, Mom said that Dad and Julie had been gone for more than an hour. "Your dad walked to the road with Julie to meet the Tysons," Mom said. "He should be back any minute."

But it wasn't Dad that I wanted to see. It was Julie. I wanted to touch her and tell her goodbye.

Dad never said what he promised Gus Tyson in exchange for Julie's transportation back to school. And I never found out for sure. But I think it had something to do with keeping Aunt Fanny Phillips in firewood. For the next four or five Sundays, Dad walked to Jubilee and cut wood all day, then racked it up in Gus Tyson's woodshed.

chapter eleven

The Monday morning that Robert and I started back to school after the Christmas holiday was bitter cold and still. A stillness that only seems to come in the dead of winter, like a promise for even colder weather in the offing.

Mom had knit mittens and a long woolen muffler for each of us for Christmas. "A blessing," I told her, as I pinned Robert's mittens to the cuffs of his jacket, so he wouldn't lose them, and buttoned the ends of his scarf inside his jacket for warmth.

I wore my muffler inside my jacket until after I got on the school bus. Then I let the ends hang loose down the front, like the other girls wore their scarfs.

Mr. Avery didn't have much to say this morning. When he rolled the window down to get rid of his chaw of tobacco, he complained of the cold and swore he was going to give up chewing. "I'm going to catch my death, if I don't," he said.

We were coming up to the crossroads at the Williams place before Mr. Avery said another word to me. "I hear that Mrs. Chally's brother, Lester Graves, has bought an interest in the farm," he said. "Lester says he's going to work it on shares with the Challys."

I had my own ideas about that, but I didn't say anything.

"What do you think of a deal like that, Seely?" Mr. Avery was asking for my honest opinion, and I hated not to answer him.

Finally, I said, "Mr. Avery, I'm not suppose to say what I think concerning Morton Chally."

"Whyever not, girl? Everybody's got a right to his own opinion."

"Dad said that I should just keep quiet. That I'd get into trouble saying what I think."

"If that's not the dangdest thing." Mr. Avery was slowing for the curve, and the Porter Hollow stop just beyond the bend in the road. "Your pa didn't say that you couldn't listen, did he?"

"No," I replied. "It's all right for me to listen, as long as I keep my mouth shut."

Mr. Avery looked at me in his mirror and smiled. "Then I'll do the talking, keeping you informed," he said, as he stopped the bus. "And you can be my silent partner."

Peedle Porter got on the bus first and slid into the

seat beside me. Annabel Grewe stopped in the aisle, her hand on the back of the seat. "Peedle, I wanted to sit by Seely, so I could talk to her."

Peedle didn't move. He didn't even look at Annabel. "Nobody's stopping you from talking," he said.

The Knight boys were crowding onto the bus, trying to squeeze by Annabel and get to a seat. "All right for you, Peedle," Annabel said, and sat down behind me.

"Write to him later, Annabel," the oldest Knight boy said. "And let us get on to the back of the bus."

"What a horribly disgusting way to start the new year," Annabel muttered. "I'm surrounded by idiots!"

After a while, her hand touched my shoulder. "I didn't mean you," she said.

I knew that. She didn't have to tell me. Last year, until Annabel Grewe had declared herself my friend, I hadn't had one. Byron Tyson and I rode the bus together, but after we got to school we seldom saw each other. I was starting my first year, and Byron was finishing his last year in high school. He was always busy with his senior class activities, and he had no time for me.

I would sit at my desk and read during the noon hour and recess, and no one ever came near me. The only time I'd leave my seat would be to go to class or the restroom. And even if I had to go to the toilet at noon, I would wait until classes took up to go. That way, there wouldn't be anyone else in the toilet at the same time as I was there.

Then one day while I was going to class, someone tripped me and I went sprawling down the hall, taking

Annabel Grewe to the floor with me. She sat up quickly, her eyes flashing angrily. "Why don't you watch where you're going?" she asked me.

"It wasn't my fault," I said, as mad as she was about it. "Somebody tripped me!"

Annabel had looked scornfully at the snickering boys lolling in the hall, and said, "Idiots! We're surrounded by idiots!"

Then she had offered her hand to help me up. "You're all skinned," she'd said, touching my peeled elbow gingerly. "Come with me. I'll take care of you."

And she had.

Now I turned with a smile to face Annabel. "That's the cross you have to bear," I teased.

She smiled, her bad humor forgotten, and we talked until the bus pulled into the schoolyard and stopped.

Ogretta Roberts and Roxie Treadwell didn't wait for Annabel and me that noon, but slipped away quietly to eat lunch together in some secret place. I didn't think anything about it, but it bothered Annabel. And when it happened the next day and the day after that, even I began to wonder. We were still friends, going to class together, and speaking in the hall, but now the closeness we'd always shared together wasn't there.

Annabel said, "I'll find out what's going on."

But she didn't. Not until way past the middle of January, when Ogretta told me what had happened to Roxie.

Roxie hadn't come to school that day, and Ogretta brought her lunchbag and ate with Annabel and me.

107

Gretta just picked at her food and hardly said a word. When Annabel got up, saying she had to go to the toilet before the bell rang, Gretta said, "Seely and I will wait for you."

As soon as Annabel was out of hearing range, Gretta said, "Roxie is afraid to ride Charlie Buskirk's bus to school. Ever since that day she met Charlie in the furnace room, Roxie has been scared to death of him. He keeps trying to get her alone again, and she's afraid he'll make her pregnant if he ever does that to her again."

Of all the things that Annabel and I had considered to be wrong, this one hadn't crossed our minds. Not at any time.

"I don't believe it," I said. "Roxie wouldn't do anything with him." Even as I said it, I wasn't really sure about that. Roxie had had a crush on Charlie Buskirk for a long time. I didn't think she'd ever meant to go that far, but after the way she had egged him on, Charlie wouldn't have taken no for an answer.

"I heard them," Gretta said, sounding close to tears. "I went to the furnace room the day Roxie was supposed to meet Charlie Buskirk. I intended to get there before he did and stay with Roxie until he got tired of waiting and went away. But he was there already."

Ogretta looked at the toes of her shoes. "You don't grow up in a house as small as ours without knowing that sound when you hear it," she said quietly.

"But Roxie said she fought him! You heard her tell it."

"She did fight him," Gretta said. "But he had his way anyhow."

I felt like crying. How could anybody hurt someone as pretty as Roxie? And that's what I asked Ogretta. "She's so pretty," I said. "How could he?"

Ogretta was as plain featured as I was, with light brown hair that just lay there. Doing what it was suppose to do. Covering her head, but nothing else for her.

"It's the pretty ones that men pick on, Seely." Then as if the thought had just come to her, Gretta said, "Annabel is pretty, too. But a man wouldn't dare to lay a hand on her. Annabel would scream her head off. Not caring who heard her. And she'd tell everybody in sight about him."

"That's what we should do about Charlie Buskirk," I said. "We ought to tell somebody."

"But who could we tell?"

I said, "We could tell Mr. Drayer. He sure fixed Elsworth Starnes's wagon when I told him Elsworth was causing trouble."

Annabel was just a few steps away, so Gretta didn't say anything then. But when the bell rang, and we separated to go to our class or study hall, she said, "I'll see you in the library during first period."

I took that to mean that we were going to talk to Mr. Drayer in his office about Charlie Buskirk and Roxie. It was a cinch we couldn't sit in the library and pretend to read while we talked about it. The room was too dim and dark to read in there. And besides, Mr. Drayer might want to use his office and we'd be in the way. But when we met in the library, I found out that Ogretta had something else on her mind.

"My folks are going to hear about this, if we tell Mr. Drayer," Gretta said. "They'll blame Roxie and say that she's fast or it wouldn't have happened. Then I won't be allowed to speak to her again," she added.

"Mom and Dad would be the same way," I said. "I'd catch old Billy hell just for knowing about it."

"We've got to think of something else," Gretta said, reaching to take down a book to look at.

"Well, what have you girls been up to now?"

Ogretta and I whirled around at the same time. Mr. Drayer's voice had startled us. We hadn't heard him come in. But there he was, resting his weight on one corner of his desk, and swinging his leg back and forth as he waited for one of us to answer him. We were there so often he just assumed we were in trouble.

"You won't pay attention to what you're told," he said. "So you're sent to me. What is it this time?"

"I don't know what you're talking about, Mr. Drayer," Gretta said. "I just came in here to get a book." She marched out the door, with me stepping close on her heels.

I expected to hear Mr. Drayer snap his fingers and order us back to the room. But he didn't.

"Gretta, let's tell Annabel," I said. "She's smart. She'd know what to do."

Ogretta shook her head. "We can't do that," she said. "Annabel talks too much. Everybody in the county would know about it before dark. And besides, that's why Roxie didn't want to eat lunch with you and Annabel. She was afraid that Annabel would see how troubled she was, and she'd get it out of her."

We were standing inside the cloakroom door, out of sight of anyone going along the hall, waiting for first period to end to go to our room.

"We could put on our coats and go to the store," I said. "No one would ever know we'd left the school, and Mrs. Avery wouldn't say anything."

Mrs. Avery was alone in the store when we walked in, and she recognized me at once. She smiled and came around to our side of the counter. "Can I sell you another pair of gloves today?"

I said, "We're not buying anything, Mrs. Avery. We're just thinking about something."

She gave us a closer look, partly puzzled, but more like one of concern. Ogretta fidgeted uncomfortably and moved a few steps away.

Ogretta was probably wishing that she had never said a word to me about Charlie Buskirk, I thought. And if it was any comfort to her, I was wishing the same thing right now.

"Anything that I can help you with?" Mrs. Avery asked.

I looked to Ogretta for support, but she was standing across the room with her back to me. If Pete Avery had been standing where his wife was, I wouldn't have hesitated a second to tell him what was bothering me. I decided that I'd just have to take the chance that Mrs. Avery was as understanding as her husband.

"There's this bus driver who . . . uh . . . forced himself on to one of the girls," I stammered. "Now she's afraid to ride the bus to school."

Mrs. Avery had drawn herself up tight, and crossed her arms on her chest. She looked cold and forbidding. I never should've told her, I thought. But I couldn't stop now.

"We didn't know who to go to about this," I said. "But somebody has to know. Somebody who will do something about it."

Mrs. Avery nodded her head. "I'll talk to Pete," she said.

Her words sent a chill all over me. "Oh, Mrs. Avery," I said. "It wasn't Mr. Avery. He's a fine man. It was that Charlie . . ."

"I know that, child." Mrs. Avery put her arm around me and stopped my babbling. "Pete will know the person to see and what to say," she explained gently. "He'll have this straightened out in no time at all."

We heard the faint sound of the dismissal bell from the school, signaling the end of the first period. Mrs. Avery put me away from her, and said, "You girls hurry back to school now and leave this trouble to Pete and me. We'll handle it."

Ogretta and I were still breathless from our fast run from the store, but we made Mr. Yoho's Ancient History class on time. No one ever knew that we had left the schoolhouse.

Two days later, Roxie came back to school. I don't know who Mr. Avery went to see, or what he had to do to get Charlie Buskirk taken off the Guthrie school bus run, but he did it. Roxie said they had a new driver the day she came back. "A grouchy old man," she said, and grinned. "He told us to sit down and shut up, or we could all walk to school." She laughed, and added, "I like him."

Now that Roxie's trouble with Charlie Buskirk had all been taken care of, and she didn't have to worry about him anymore, Roxie was lighthearted and pleasant to be with again. We four ate our lunch together, splitting the contents of the brown paper bags four ways, and our hopes and dreams as well.

I told Annabel everything, as soon as I knew it, but I made her promise with her right hand to God, that she would never tell another living soul. "If you do," I said, "the rest of us will swear it never happened."

Annabel pouted for all of five minutes and pretended to be hurt to think I wouldn't trust her with a secret. "I talk a lot," she said, "but I don't really say anything."

chapter twelve

Mr. Avery never did mention Charlie Buskirk to me or ask who the girl was that he had molested. And I expected him to. It seemed only natural to me that he would wonder about it, especially a man as curious as Mr. Avery.

He sure showed enough interest and curiosity about what was going on at the Williams place. One morning he said, "Seely, I guess Lester Graves must have come into some money. He's bought himself a pickup truck. I've seen it at the Williams farm for the past three days now."

A few days later as we passed there, Mr. Avery said, "Lester must still be visiting his sister. The truck's not gone yet." He slowed the school bus down to a crawl and craned his neck to get a closer look at the place.

"Seely, it's dang funny," he said. "Up to the day that boy got shot, Lester Graves had no use at all for Morton Chally. Barely passed the time of day with him when they met. But seems like now, the two of them are thicker than a pack of sheep-killing dogs."

Mr. Avery didn't talk to me after the other kids got on the bus, only on the long stretch of road from where I got on to where he made the next stop at Porter Hollow road, in the morning, and when we were alone on the bus going home at night. Generally, he did all the talking, and I just listened. Most of the things he said didn't require an answer, so I made none.

One night at the supper table Dad was telling Mom what the WPA crew had done that day. He had said all along that the work the county found for them to do was a waste of time and money. But since that was what they wanted him to do to earn his twelve dollars and fifty cents a week, he'd do it.

"We worked on that little side road that borders the Williams place today," Dad said. "Filling in the chuckholes and making the road fit for folks to get to Needmore on it."

Robert laughed. "Needmore," he said. "Needmore what?"

Dad chuckled and said from the looks of the town it needed more of everything than it had. Then he turned to Mom and said, "Speaking of need, the Challys must be getting hard up and feeling the pinch. Looks like they've sold all their cows and their plowhorses. We worked that stretch of road from daylight till dark today, and I didn't see one head of livestock on the place."

I forgot that I was suppose to be Mr. Avery's silent partner. I was filled to the brim with the things he had told me, and now that Dad had brought up the Chally name, I couldn't wait to tell him what I knew about them.

"Mr. Avery says there's something funny going on at the Williams place," I blurted out. "Lester Graves has bought a new pickup truck and moved in there with Onalee and Chally." I stopped to catch my breath, then went on. "Mr. Avery said that before the accident, Lester wouldn't have a thing to do with Morton Chally. But now they're thicker than thieves."

"It seems to me," Dad said, "that you and Mr. Avery have been doing a mighty lot of talking these days." He looked at me and frowned. "Seely, have you been trying to stir up trouble against Morton Chally by telling Mr. Avery your suspicions and the things you've imagined that he's done?"

"I haven't said anything," I told Dad. "Mr. Avery asked me what I thought. But I told him I wasn't suppose to say what I thought of Morton Chally. And I haven't," I added hastily.

"Well, see that you don't," Dad said. "There's enough speculation going around about them people as it is."

That was the end of it, as far as Dad was concerned. He turned to Mom and went on from where I had interrupted him, to tell her of his work. I listened for a while, but when he didn't mention the Williams place, I closed my ears and did some speculating about it on my own.

I figured that if other people besides Mr. Avery and myself were wondering about the strange goings-on at the Williams farm, sooner or later they would find out the truth about Morton Chally.

The next morning as the school bus approached the crossroad at the Williams farm, I leaned forward over Mr. Avery's shoulder as if I was looking to see Dad and the others working on the side road.

"Dad worked along there yesterday," I said. "He told Mom that he didn't see one head of livestock on that farm, from the time they started work until quitting time."

Mr. Avery slapped his hand hard on the steering wheel. "By dang, Seely. I knew there was something puzzling me about that place, and that's what it was. I've seen no cows or horses around the barn lately."

I sat back in my seat, and Mr. Avery tilted his head to smile at me in the rearview mirror.

"Seely, you're a card," he said. "A regular ace in the hole when it comes to winning a bet."

"What did you bet on, Mr. Avery?"

His eyes sought mine in the mirror again, then went quickly back to the road ahead of us. "About the same thing you did," he answered. "I'm betting that the shotgun that killed Russell Williams never slipped out of Morton Chally's hand by mistake. And that Uncle Lester knows it."

117

I shivered and drew my overall jacket closer around me. It gave me the chills to hear Mr. Avery put into words the thing I had been thinking all along. I was glad when the bus stopped at Porter Hollow road and Peedle slid into the seat, close beside me.

The days started getting warmer after the first week of February. Annabel and Roxie would meet Ogretta and me at the Avery's store, and we'd eat our lunch in the school bus every day that Mr. Avery left it parked there. Since the day that Gretta and I had gone to the store to talk to Mrs. Avery about Charlie Buskirk, we had gotten to be good friends with her. One day Mrs. Avery brought a pan of fresh-baked cupcakes out to the school bus for us girls. She said that her and Pete would never eat them all. They would just go stale. "You girls would be doing me a favor if you'd take them off my hands," she said.

We were glad to help her out. We each took a cupcake for our lunch and saved one to eat at the last recess. "We'll be hungry again by then," Annabel said. Mrs. Avery smiled and took the empty pan back to the store.

We were just two days away from the Valentine Day Sweetheart Dance at school. Ogretta and I weren't going to the dance, but Annabel and Roxie were going and that's all they could talk about. Annabel said that her mother had this simply gorgeous dinner dress, and she was making it over to fit her for the dance. Roxie was going to wear the same dress she had worn last year. "And the year before that." She laughed.

118

Ogretta had been invited to a party that a friend of one of her brother's was giving that night, and she wouldn't be at the Sweetheart Dance. "It's just as well," Gretta said. "I've got two left feet, when it comes to dancing."

Annabel said, "Seely, I wish you'd change your mind and go to the dance with Roxie and me. You'd have fun, once you were there."

I shook my head. I wasn't interested in dancing. I wouldn't have wanted to go even if I'd had a new dress and slippers to wear to it. Maybe if I was sixteen, like Annabel and Roxie, I could get excited about going to a dance. But right now, the party Ogretta was going to on the back end of a hay-filled truck sounded like more fun than a Sweetheart Dance. But I hadn't been asked to go on the hayride.

I beat Robert home from school on Friday evening. He came in clutching a handful of brightly colored paper hearts and a few stiff and shiny boughten valentines. He spread them proudly on the table to show Mom and me how many he had.

"Where's your valentines, Seely?" he asked. "Didn't you get any?"

"We don't give valentines in high school. That's for children."

Robert chose to ignore my superior tone. If he even noticed. "Miss Etta helped us make a valentine box," he said. "And all week we've been making valentines to put in there. After school today, when Miss Etta opened the box, this many of them were mine."

Mom exclaimed over the pretty valentines, sorting through them with her fingers and counting them as she she did so. "My lands, Robert," she said. "You've got twenty-four valentines."

"That's how many kids there are in school," he said. "And all of us had to make a valentine for everyone or bring one from home. Like these," he said, pointing to the store-boughten ones.

"Well! No wonder you—"

"Seely," Mom said, shaking her head above Robert. "Leave him to his pretties and go bring me an armload of firewood."

Later when Dad came home, Mom said to Robert, "Bring your pretty valentines and show your daddy how many you got from the kids at school."

Robert's chin touched his chest, and he wouldn't look at her. "Everybody got one," he said in a low voice. "They were just old pieces of colored paper, so I put them in the stove and burned them."

Dad said, "Why, son . . ."

Robert started crying and ran from the room.

"What's wrong with the boy?" Dad asked. "Why would he burn his valentines, and then cry about it?"

Mom said, "He was so proud of them, Rob. I can't imagine where he got the notion that they were worthless things."

I left the room quietly, so as not to draw attention to my going, and went to the bedroom I shared with Robert. I hadn't meant to belittle his boodle of valentines, or to make them seem less a treasure to keep, just because everyone else in the room got the same number of valentines as he did.

Robert was lying face down on his bed, his arms crossed under his head, with scraps of red paper showing from beneath his pillow. "Robert." I spoke his name softly, then sat down on the bed beside him.

He was awfully small for his age, I thought. It seemed to me that Jamie had been a lot bigger when he was eight. But then, I'd only been nine, going on ten, at the time, and I could be wrong about his size.

I put my hand on Robert's head and smoothed the roached-up cowlick that Mom said was caused by a double crown. "Robert, you didn't really burn your valentines, did you?"

He moved his head from side to side, but he didn't say anything.

"Then why did you tell Dad you had?" I asked softly.

He turned over on the bed and looked at me, his face still streaked with tears. "I aimed to," he said. "You didn't get any valentines, and you weren't glad that I did."

I wanted to hug him, to tell him that I'd been glad for him, but the defensive, almost accusing, tone of his voice held me back.

"I wanted you to be proud of me," Robert said. "But because the other kids got as many as I did, you thought I wasn't anyone special at all."

"Oh, Robert," I said, bending to lay my face close to his tear-stained one. "You're my brother. You'd be spe-

121

cial to me whether you gone one, or a hundred and one valentines. Don't you know that, silly?"

His arms crept up slowly until they hugged my neck. I lifted him to a sitting position, but he didn't take his arms away. So I sat and held him close.

"Supper will be ready soon," I said, rocking him gently back and forth. "You wash your face, so you'll look like Robert again, and after we eat, we'll show Dad all your pretty valentines."

Robert drew away from me, his eyes wide and a little bit scared. "We can't do that, Seely," he said, as if I was slightly feebleminded. "I've done told Dad I'd burned them."

"When I tell him that I stopped you from putting them in the stove, Dad will understand. He knows that people intend to do a lot of things that they don't do," I said. "And sometimes they say they have, when they haven't yet."

I slid off the bed and reached for Robert's hand. "Come," I said gently. "We'll go together, and everything will be all right."

And it was.

chapter thirteen

"There was a nasty wreck out south of town Saturday night," Mr. Avery told me, as soon as I got on the bus. "A truckload of school kids, out on a hayride, got rear-ended by another truck. No one was hurt bad," he added quickly, as I gasped with horror. "But kids and hay was scattered along a quarter mile of Dixie highway."

"My friend, Ogretta Roberts, was supposed to be on that hayride," I said. "I don't suppose you heard—"

"All I heard about it, Seely, was that a couple of the girls were dangling their legs from the end of the hay-filled flatbed truck when the other one hit it. I didn't hear their names, but they're in the hospital in Louisville right now. The doctors are trying to save their legs."

I didn't notice when we passed the Williams place. I was looking ahead to where I stepped off the bus in the schoolyard and would see Ogretta running to meet me.

There were several girls going on that hayride, I told myself. It could be any one of them. Just because Gretta was on the truck, it didn't mean that she would be one of the girls sitting on the very back end of it.

But when Annabel Grewe got on the bus and pushed Peedle out of the way with a shaky, "I'm sitting with Seely today," I knew that one of the girls was Ogretta. Only deep concern for a friend would ever shake Annabel Grewe this much.

"Mother is driving to Louisville today," Annabel said. "She's taking Gretta's mom to the hospital." Then in a voice shaking with rage at the injustice of it, she said, "A stinking hayride! Can you believe it? Gretta may never walk again, just because she went on one stinking hayride!"

We learned from Annabel's mother that the doctors did three operations on Ogretta's legs that first week. The next week an infection developed, and Annabel's mother said that the doctors had to stop their patching and sewing and give all their attention to fighting the infection to keep it from spreading.

Roxie cried every time Annabel passed on Mrs. Grewe's reports about Ogretta's progress. But I didn't cry. And neither did Annabel. Annabel was still too angry, too outraged that this could happen to Gretta, to cry about it. I knew that crying couldn't change what had happened. It never had for me. And it wouldn't help Gretta get well any faster. So I saved my tears.

After a while, one of Ogretta's brothers came to school and cleaned out her desk, taking her books and papers home with him. The very next day her desk was moved to the back of the room. In the classes I had taken with Ogretta, the teachers announced that Ogretta Roberts wouldn't be coming back to class. "She will be in the hospital for a long time yet," they said. "And a greater time before she will be able to attend school again."

Roxie said, "Doesn't it seem odd not to have Gretta here? She didn't say much, and she hardly ever did anything to speak of. But she sure added something, didn't she?"

We were eating lunch at the time in Mr. Avery's school bus. There had been a cold drizzle of rain all morning, and now it was coming down harder, sounding more like hail or sleet as it hit the metal roof of the bus.

"She sure did," Annabel answered, taking the last half of sandwich, and speaking loudly to be heard over the rattle of rain on the roof. "Gretta brought good homemade yeast bread, with something on it besides peanut butter."

I smiled at the two of them. "Mom puts peanut butter on a dry biscuit for my lunch to punish me," I said.

Annabel put on a face of pure horror. "Good Lord, Seely. What have you done to deserve that?"

"Nothing." I laughed. "That's just in case I do misbehave."

We waited in the school bus, hoping that the sleet would slack off so we could get back to school. Finally, when we could wait no longer, we made a run for it. I got soaked to the skin and spent the next hour in study hall shivering and shaking while my clothes dried on me.

My denim jacket was dry when I put it on that evening to go home. But before I could get on the bus, it was wet again. Mr. Avery said that the rain had started to freeze on the windshield, but so far the roads were passable.

"You kids had better get a move on," he yelled at the ones up front who were holding up traffic, "or this bus will be froze solid to the ground, and we'll have to sit here."

The bus made the stop at the Otises, and the next two stops, without any trouble. But after that even when Mr. Avery geared it down and barely touched the brakes, the back end of the bus would slip and slide sideways before we came to a complete stop.

When Mr. Avery stopped at Porter Hollow Road, Peedle said, "Mr. Avery, trying to drive is getting worse all the time. How will you get home?"

Pete Avery scratched his head under his cap. "I'll tell you, son. If it gets too bad, I'll bunk in at Seely's tonight."

My stop was the next and last one on the route.

Peedle Porter looked at me, then back to Mr. Avery. "You are welcome to stay at our house," he said. "If you can make it this far."

Mr. Avery thanked Peedle, then warned him of the ice on the steps. But his warning came too late. Peedle was already picking himself up from the roadside. Peedle brushed at his britches, then walked carefully across the road, in front of the bus, and started up the lane toward home.

The oldest Knight boy helped Annabel down the steps of the bus, then holding onto each other they left the road and started slowly climbing the hill, sliding back two steps for every one they took forward.

Mr. Avery turned the heater fan up as high as it would go to keep the ice off the windshield, and the bus crept slowly down the road toward my stop.

"It looks like February is giving March a headstart this year," Mr. Avery said.

There was nothing I could say to that. Two days until the month of March, and already it was showing itself.

"Of course, February being what it is," he went on, "this ice storm could pass and the sun come up on a clear day tomorrow."

"I've heard Dad say that a day never passes in February but what it thaws somewhere."

I could see Mr. Avery's face through the rearview mirror, and he was smiling. "I believe that's right," Seely," he said seriously.

As we passed the Williams place, Mr. Avery motioned toward the house. "Haven't seen a sign of life around there for a week now," he said.

The place looked deserted. It was dark enough to have a lamp lighted, but there was no light showing anywhere in the house.

"Mrs. Avery saw Onalee at the railroad depot the first of the week," he said. "But she didn't find out if Mrs. Chally was coming or going or just meeting someone coming in on the train."

I didn't wish Onalee Chally any more grief than she'd had already. But I did most desperately want to see her husband brought to account for what he had done to Onalee's son, Russell Williams. "I hope she was taking the train as far away from here as she can get," I said.

Mr. Avery nodded his head approvingly. He had to give his full attention to his driving then, and no more was said about the Challys.

The bus slid to a stop at the end of my road, and with a "Watch your step, Seely," from Mr. Avery, and my answer, "I'll see you Monday," the bus door closed and the bus went creeping on up the road.

I moved to the weeds and dead grass that bordered the dirt road. The ice wasn't frozen as solid on the grasses, and it broke easily under my feet as I tramped up the hill, over the ridge, and down the other side to the house.

Dad wasn't home yet, and Mom was nearly frantic with worry. "He should've come home this afternoon," she said, "as soon as it started sleeting." She walked the floor, pausing now and then to listen for Dad's step on the back porch.

So as not to worry Mom more than she was already, Robert and I did the chores without being told to do them. We carried in firewood and filled the woodboxes in the front room as well as the kitchen. Then we brought in water for the stove reservoir and a bucketful for drinking and cooking. When there was nothing more to be done, we got into dry clothes, and hung our damp things to dry behind the kitchen stove.

"I'm hungry," Robert said. "It's time we ate supper."

128

"We'll wait for your daddy," Mom said shortly.

"Clearing drainage ditches and culverts in this kind of weather," Mom said, adding more wood to the already red-hot cookstove. "And him without a raincoat of any kind or rubber boots to keep himself dry."

She moved the teakettle to the hottest spot on the stove. "I'll make Rob some hot sassafras tea," she said to herself. "I've got some roots put away, just in case."

Dad stumbled into the house a short while later and fell into a chair. His clothes were near to being frozen on his body, but he didn't seem to know, or even care, as long as he didn't have to move another step further.

Mom stripped Dad's stiff, wet coat and shoes off him, then she ordered me from the room. "Bring me the quilt from my bed," Mom said. "And be quick about it."

I stripped the quilt from her bed faster than I thought possible and hurried back to the kitchen. Mom met me in the doorway, whipped the quilt from my hands, and she had it wrapped around Dad before I got to him.

"Seely, the tea is ready. Pour your daddy a cup and add extra sugar. He needs it," Mom said, her voice soft and low.

Dad had his eyes closed, but as Mom spooned the tea into his mouth, tears slipped from beneath the lids and slid down his face. Dad started to raise his hand, to wipe his face, I guess. But then he let his hand drop to his lap, as though he was too tired to make the effort.

While Mom fed Dad the sassafras tea and the hot broth from the beef and noodles she had made for supper, I took the hot flatirons from the stove, wrapped

129

them in pieces of old flannel, and put them at the foot of their bed so it would be warm for Dad.

Robert and I ate a bowl of beef and noodles, then Mom sent us to bed. I don't know what time it was when she went to bed. Or even if she ever did. She woke me a couple of times during the night. Once while she was building up the fire in the heating stove in the front room and again when she came into my bedroom to get more covers to put over Dad.

The next morning, Dad was out of his head with a fever, and not able to get out of bed. Mom bathed his face and hands with cold water to bring down the fever, then she had to pile every quilt and blanket in the house over him when he started chilling and wouldn't quit.

This went on all day Saturday and most of Sunday. Then late Sunday evening, Dad said he felt better, like getting up. "Just like to sit in the kitchen and smoke my pipe for a while," he said.

Mom fussed at him, said he could sit up in bed. She'd even bring him his pipe. "But you ought to stay still," she said. "Not get in a draft."

But when he insisted, Mom helped him to a chair near the kitchen stove, and tucked a quilt around him. "Good diddly-damn, woman," Dad said, his voice a weak shadow of his usual tone, "stop hovering over me like I was an invalid."

"I've just had a bout with chills and fever," Dad mumbled. "Not double-pneumonia."

"Rob, we've been married near to twenty-five years," Mom said, "and there's never been a day that you haven't

130

done your best for me. Now, you just behave yourself and let me take care of you for a day or so."

Dad turned his head to look up at Mom. She closed her eyes and bent forward, putting her face against his rough, unshaven cheek. For a long moment neither one of them moved or said a word. Then Mom's lips moved to touch Dad's lightly, before she drew away. They seemed to have forgotten that Robert and I were in the room.

Late that night, Mom shook me awake. "Get up, Seely," she said urgently. "Your daddy has taken a bad turn, and you've got to go to Jubilee for Gus Tyson. Tell him to send a doctor, Seely. Then you hurry back here."

I heard the words, "Your daddy has taken a bad turn," and I was out of bed, throwing on whatever came to hand. When I was leaving the house, Mom stopped me. "Rap on Nellie's door as you go by. Tell her we need Mr. Paully."

"The preacher? What do we need him for?"

"Just do as I say, Seely. And hurry!"

I took off running through the ice-covered field and over the hill toward Nellie's house, my feet slipping and sliding from under me with every step. I'd taken this shortcut so many times that I thought I could walk it with my eyes shut. But I couldn't run it through the pitch black of night, not and stay on the ice-glazed path.

I floundered into the trees and wild berry briars, then found my way back to the path and ran some more. The trail down the other side of the hill was wider and more clearly marked. I could run awhile, walk to catch my breath, and know I was headed in the right direction.

Nellie must have heard me coming. I had no more than touched the door when it opened and Nellie stood there.

"Why, it's Seely." She reached for my hand to take me inside. "You're freezing cold," she said. "Come, get warm."

I'd got my wind back, and I could speak now. "Mom said to tell you that we need Mr. Paully at our house, right away."

I turned to leave. "Seely, what's wrong?"

"Dad's real bad, Nellie. I'm going for Gus Tyson to get a doctor."

"Mr. Paully will go to your dad," Nellie said. "Don't you worry."

It was gravel road from Nellie's to where Gus Tyson lived with his sister, Aunt Fanny Phillips, and I made it there in no time at all. I got them out of bed, and they took me back home. But we couldn't reach a doctor. He wouldn't have been needed by the time he got there anyway. While I was running through the night, trying to get help for him, Dad had died.

Julie came home for Dad's funeral. Gus Tyson met her in Oolitic and brought her home.

It was after dark when they got to the house. She hugged Mom and cried. Then the two of them went into the little room at the foot of the stairs to see Dad. They stayed in the room with Dad for a long time.

132

I gave Robert his supper, then he went to bed. After a while, I went to bed too. But I didn't sleep right away.

It seemed like all night long I dozed and woke up every few minutes. And every time I awoke, I could hear the low murmur of Mom's and Julie's voices as they talked. I couldn't hear what they were saying, just the sound of their voices.

Once during the night, I heard Mom or Julie, I couldn't tell which, crying as though her heart was breaking. I buried my face in the pillow and cried my heart out for them.

Julie told me later that they had talked the night away. "Seely, I never really understood or knew Mom until we started talking," she said.

I think Mom must have felt the same way about Julie. She turned to her for everything. I took care of Robert and saw to his needs, and Julie comforted Mom. We didn't have a chance to console each other. Not until the day we buried Dad.

The field behind the Baptist church, where the people of Oolitic kept their dead, was wide open to the cold winds that swept across country that first day of March. And while the Reverend Mr. Paully was reading over Dad's open grave, the wind brought to us the sound of taps being played for another burial on the far side of the cemetery. Julie squeezed my hand till it hurt. But I didn't let on. The hurt in my hand was a small thing compared to all the pain contained in that cold, windy, field.

133

chapter fourteen

After the funeral, Gus Tyson came to the house to take Julie to Oolitic to get the bus back to Terre Haute and her school. Mom clung to Julie as if she couldn't bear to let her go. "Stay," she begged. "Stay with me."

"I've got to go, Mom. I'll miss my bus." Julie gave Mom a quick kiss, then moved toward the car. Robert and I had already said our goodbyes to Julie. We were just waiting to wave her on her way. "Take care of yourself," she said to Mom, "and look after the kids." She got in the car, waved once, then never looked back.

I had never felt so alone as I waved goodbye to Julie. Then I stood and watched until the car went out of sight over the ridge. I knew it was harder for her to leave than it was for me to stay behind. But just for a moment, in my loneliness, I envied Julie the going.

134

Mom turned her face from the road and came slowly back to the house. Robert and I waited until she opened the door, then we followed her inside. Without a word, Mom went straight to her bedroom and closed her door.

I put wood on the hot coals in the cookstove, then set about making our supper, just as I'd been doing for the past couple of days. Robert brought in wood and kindling for the kitchen stove, but the large chunks of wood that were used in the heating stove in the front room were too heavy for him to handle. I carried the big pieces of wood to the porch, where they'd be handy to get to, then helped Robert bring in water to last the night.

When supper was ready and on the table, I went to Mom's bedroom door and called her.

"I'm not hungry," she said. "You and Robert go ahead and eat your supper."

"Mom, come on to the table," I said. "You'll feel better after you eat something."

"Seely, I'll eat when I'm hungry," she said irritably. "Now, go away and leave me alone!"

I left her alone.

Robert and I cleaned up the kitchen after supper, then I banked the fires in the kitchen and front room stoves, and we went to bed.

Robert shook me awake in the middle of the night. "Seely, is it time to get up and go to school yet?"

I looked at the clock that I had brought in from the kitchen. "Robert, it's hours yet till we have to get up. Now go back to sleep," I told him.

He stood beside my bed for a moment, shivering in his thin pajamas. "You'll get me up for school, won't you?" he asked. "I don't want to stay at home any more."

I promised him that I would. He crawled back into bed, and he was sound asleep a few minutes later. But I lay awake for hours afterwards, not able to go back to sleep.

Mom wasn't up yet, when I went to the kitchen the next morning. I built a fire in the stove, put on the coffee-pot for Mom and made breakfast for Robert and myself. When Robert and I left for school, Mom still hadn't stirred from her bedroom.

Pete Avery's school bus was waiting at the end of the road, the heater going and the bus warm when I got there. He closed the door, then sat a moment before putting the bus in gear and moving on. Finally, he looked at me and said real solemnly, "I was mighty sorry to hear about your pa, Seely."

I answered him just as solemnly. "Thank you, Mr. Avery."

Nothing else was said about it.

When we passed the Williams place, we both turned our heads to look at the house. But neither one of us said a word.

At the first stop past the crossroads, Annabel Grewe got on the bus. She looked at me and I scooted over to make room for her on the seat beside me. But she lowered her eyes and went on past me to the seat directly behind me.

Peedle Porter slid quickly into the seat next to me. He smiled, and said, "Hi, Seely. I missed you."

I said, "Hi yourself, Peedle. What's been going on since I've seen you?"

"Ah," he said. "Let me think." After a moment of what appeared to be deep thought, Peedle started reciting a long list of happenings and marking them off on his fingers.

When Peedle had run out of fingers and got quiet, I turned in my seat to speak to Annabel. She seemed uncomfortable, as if she didn't know what to say to me, and she wished I would go away and not bother her. It was as though I was suddenly deformed in some way, and she didn't want to see it. The one time her eyes met mine, hers filled with pity, and she quickly looked away.

I got the same treatment at school. Everybody looked at me, but when I smiled or started to speak to them, they quickly turned away. Even the teachers spoke to me as if I'd had a long siege of sickness.

At noontime, as they were getting their coats on to go to lunch, I cornered Roxie and Annabel in the cloakroom.

"What's wrong with you two?" I demanded to know. "I'm the same as I was on Friday. You liked me then. Now you act like I've got leprosy. Like you are afraid you'll catch it by talking to me."

Roxie started crying. "I'm not mad at you. I'm just so sorry for you, and I don't know what to say," she blubbered.

Annabel said, "Hush, Roxie. You'll make Seely cry." Then she said to me, "I thought you might want to be left alone, the first day back, and all." She looked at the floor, then at Roxie, and finally at me. "Seely, I didn't talk to you because I didn't know what to say, either," Annabel said softly.

"You don't have to tell me how sorry you feel about my dad. I'd be just as sorry if you stood in my place."

I stopped and waited for one of them to speak. To say something, anything, to let me know that having a death in the family couldn't change things between us. But they just stood there, their eyes on the floor. Neither one of them spoke.

"I didn't know that I would lose my friends," I said, "when I lost my dad."

My voice broke. I reached blindly for my jacket, wanting to get away from them, but Annabel caught me in her arms and held me.

When the crying was over and the same handkerchief had dried all our tears, Annabel said, "I feel better now," and kind of laughed. "I could probably force myself to eat something, if either one of you have anything I like in your brown bag."

We ate outside, huddled together in the chimney corner and shielding each other from the cold wind.

"Have you heard any news of Gretta?" I asked. "Is she getting better?"

"Mother went to the hospital Monday," Annabel replied. "Gretta told Mother that the doctors were going to start skin grafts this week. And if the grafted skin takes hold and heals the way it should, she'll be able to get out of bed soon. Would you believe," Annabel said incredulously, "Ogretta is actually looking forward to the day she can be on crutches?"

I nodded my head. I could believe it. "Gretta would see the crutches as just another stepping-stone toward being able to walk on her own again," I said.

"It's a stinking shame that it's taking so long for Gretta," Annabel said. "The other girl who was hurt that night came home a couple of weeks ago."

Roxie shivered and said she was freezing her butt off. We should eat now and talk later. We finished our lunch and hurried back inside where she could get warm.

Having Annabel and Roxie walking with me, talking and laughing naturally, made all the difference in the way the other kids looked at me.

When I laughed out loud in Mr. Yoho's Ancient History class, he looked shocked for a moment. Then he smiled, and from then on he seemed more at ease around me.

As Peedle Porter was getting ready to leave the bus that evening, he turned and looked soberly at me. "My dad said I was supposed to tell you," he said. "We are sorry about Mr. Robinson. He was a fine man. I'd have told you this morning, but I didn't want to remind you of it, first thing."

I said, "Peedle, tell your dad we appreciate you all thinking of us."

"I'll do it," he said. And left the bus.

Mr. Avery shook his head. "A great heart and the mind of a child," he said to himself. And we went on toward home.

The fire in the cookstove had gone out, and supper hadn't even been started. The kitchen was cold, like an empty house, and when I called Mom my voice sounded hollow. I pulled my jacket closer around me and went on toward the front room.

Mom was sitting in the rocking chair, close by the heating stove. She had her coat on and a scarf tied over her head as if she was ready to go somewhere.

Robert came out of our bedroom and stood quietly beside me. "She was sitting there when I got home," he said, so low that I could barely hear him. "I thought she was . . . asleep. You know, like Dad was asleep."

"Mom is all right, Robert," I said quietly. "She's just worn out and tired from all she's had to do these past few days."

I felt the heating stove. It was stone cold. I got a blanket to put over Mom, then I motioned for Robert to come to the kitchen with me.

"I'll build a big fire in the cookstove," I told Robert. "And that will help to heat the front room. There'll be time to fix the fire in there after Mom wakes up."

Robert watched me as I shook the grates, then carried the ashes outside so there would be no chance of a hot coal in the stove. Then I loaded the firebox with kindling and dry wood, poured kerosene over it all, and struck a match to it. Within minutes, the fire was roaring up the chimney and the lids on top of the stove were red hot.

I was stirring up pancakes for our supper when Mom came to the kitchen. She had a dazed look about her, as if she still wasn't fully awake. She glanced at her coat and raised her hand to touch the headscarf. "I was going outside to chop firewood," she said. "But I must have fallen asleep."

I smiled at her. "Take off your coat and hat," I said, "and stay awhile. Supper will be ready in a minute."

Mom kind of smiled and left the room. But she was back almost at once. "Seely, the fire is out in the heating stove. It's like a barn in there."

"I know," I said. "You were sleeping so sound that I didn't want to wake you by messing with the stove."

"But we need a fire in there." She started out of the kitchen, mumbling something under her breath.

"I'll fix it later, Mom. After we have supper."

That seemed to satisfy her. After she had taken off her coat and freshened up a bit, she came to the table and ate pancakes with Robert and me. She even commented that I could make better pancakes than she could. That wasn't true. But it made us both feel good. Her, to say it, and me, to hear it.

After that evening, there wasn't much to make either one of us feel good. Once in a great while, I would come home from school to a warm, clean house and supper cooking on the stove. But not often. Most of the time, I'd get home to find Robert carrying in any kind of wood he could lay his hands on, the fire in the kitchen stove just a bed of coals or dead ashes. Mom would be in her bedroom with the door locked or sitting in a daze,

141

rocking in the rocking chair beside a cold heating stove.

One evening I got home just in time to stop Robert from pouring kerosene on wood that he had laid over the hot coals, trying to start a fire in the cookstove.

"Don't you ever do that!" I screamed at him. "It could explode and kill you! The house could burn down and leave us homeless." I was scared so bad I was ready to cry. "That's all we'd need to top off this miserable winter," I said furiously. "Everything else has already happened!"

Robert's eyes got big and tear-filled, and he backed away from me. He looked as if he was scared to death, like the last person he could count on had turned on him. I stopped yelling and slumped down in a chair.

"I was trying to start a fire," he said, crying now. "I just wanted to help you."

"Oh, honey," I said, holding my hands out to him. "I'm sorry I yelled at you. You do your part bringing in the wood," I told him, gently. "From now on, you leave the stoves and starting fires to me."

Mom called, "Seely," and came in from the front room. "What are you screaming about? They can hear you clear into Jubilee."

"If Robert had poured that kerosene onto those hot coals, like he was starting to do," I said, "they could have heard this house blowing up too!"

"You don't have to shout at him about it," she said peevishly. She picked up a stick of wood and turned toward the stove.

I had been scared out of my wits, and now I felt that

Mom was finding fault with me for the way I had handled things.

"I wouldn't have had to scream at Robert," I said, "if you'd been out here where you belong, instead of laying around in bed all day. Robert and me, we can't do everything."

Mom whirled to face me, her brown eyes flashing with anger, and the stick of wood raised above her head like a club. "You speak to me again like that, and I'll knock you across the room."

She seemed surprised to suddenly realize that she was holding the firewood in her hand. She turned and put it in the stove.

"Go on, and get your chores done," Mom said, her voice low. "I'll make our supper tonight."

I was still wearing my cap and jacket. I put on my mittens and went outside to split wood. Robert came out soon afterwards and stood nearby, waiting until I had cut an armload for him to take back to the house.

I scream at Robert, I thought. Mom screams at me. And only God knows what is screaming at Mom to make her act the way she does lately.

I raised Dad's two-bladed axe above my head and brought it down squarely, with all my strength, on the chunk of wood, splitting it neatly in the middle. Then I quartered the halves and quartered them again to make the pieces fit in the cookstove. Robert stood quietly by, watching me.

143

chapter fifteen

Mom didn't get up the next morning. I made our breakfast, and Robert and I left for school at the same time. The days were getting longer and daylight came a lot earlier. They were warmer too. It was still cold, but not the bitter, biting cold that we'd had up to now.

"I may stop in at Nellie's house, coming home from school," Robert said, and looked to me for permission.

"Don't stay too late," I said.

He brushed the hair out of his eyes and smiled. Then he hurried off across the field for school.

Robert needed a haircut, I thought, as I watched him go. His hair was down over his ears, nearly to his collar in back, and it seemed always in his eyes in front. I'd have to see if Aunt Fanny could cut it for him Saturday.

As I went along, I arranged our time for the coming weekend. Do the washing early, so it could be drying while I cleaned the house. Take Robert to get a haircut. Clean the kitchen cabinet on Sunday to make room for the food stuff that Aunt Fanny would bring us from the Welfare on Monday. Since Dad had been gone, and Mom wasn't doing much of the cooking any more, we had Welfare stuff left over on the shelf from week to week.

"Thought you were going to walk right on by me," Mr. Avery said, as I got on the bus. "Your mind appeared to be a million miles away."

"No, not that far away," I said, "just a couple of days."

He cleared his throat and started whistling quietly through his teeth. Mr. Avery did a lot of throat clearing and whistling since he had given up chewing tobacco. I hardly ever noticed it any longer. But it seemed that he had a purpose for it this morning.

"The house on the Williams place caught fire during the night," he said, "and burned to the ground."

I opened my mouth to tell him how near we had been to having a fire at our house last night, then closed it.

"What were you going to say, Seely?"

I looked up and caught Mr. Avery watching me in the rearview mirror. "Nothing, Mr. Avery," I said. "I was just thinking."

It wouldn't do to tell anyone about the way things were at our house. As soon as Mom got well of whatever it was ailing her, and I figured it was just being poor and having to take welfare, it would shame her to know that others knew about it. Not that I thought Mr. Avery would ever repeat anything I told him, but I'd feel funny having him know of our family troubles.

"It beats me how that fire got started at the Williamses' house," Mr. Avery went on. "No one's been living there since Onalee packed up and went to Pittsburgh."

"Did she really go away, Mr. Avery? I've wished and wished that she would go."

"Then you got your wish, Seely," he replied. His eyes smiled at me from the mirror. "Mrs. Avery always liked Onalee too," he said. "She asked Jake at the railroad station about her. Jake said that he sold Mrs. Chally a ticket to Pittsburgh and saw her get on the train himself."

The house was still smoking and smoldering as we went by there. Two cars, one with the sheriff's star on the door, were parked in the driveway, and a panel truck sat in the barnlot.

"Wonder why all the cars are there?" I asked, looking back at the place.

"Never can tell," Mr. Avery answered. "But I'll see what I can find out today, Seely, and let you know."

During all the time that Mr. Avery and I had been keeping our eyes on the Williams place, trying to find something that we could hold against Morton Chally, he had never mentioned it after the other kids got on the bus. And he didn't talk about the fire today.

I hadn't told Annabel and Roxie of our suspicions. That was another thing I kept to myself. Russell's name hadn't been mentioned between us since the week after Thanksgiving. There was no reason for Annabel and Roxie to believe that I ever thought of Russell Williams now-a-days. I felt like I had become the silent partner in a secret corporation that Mr. Avery and I hadn't really intended to form.

That evening after the last one had left the bus at Porter Hollow, and we were on our way home, Mr. Avery said, "Getting information out of some folks is like pulling hen's teeth."

I smiled to myself. I thought that Mr. Avery could be pretty close-mouthed himself, when he wanted to be.

"But I did find out that that fire was set on purpose," he said. "Now, as our friend Peedle would say, do you want to know why someone deliberately started that fire?"

"Mr. Avery, stop teasing, and tell me what you know,"

He turned in his seat to look at me, and his face was dead serious. "I'm not sure I ought to, Seely," he said, turning back to watch the road. "It's not a pleasant thing for a young girl to hear."

I didn't say anything. I knew he wouldn't go back on his word. He'd said he would find out and tell me, and he would.

"When the ashes had cooled," he said, "the remains of a man's body was found in them. I guess the fire was supposed to do away with it, but there was enough left to identify as a man."

"Lester Graves," I said. "I'll bet you."

"That's the way I figure it," Mr. Avery said. "Even allowing for the fire, the body's not big enough to have been Morton Chally."

As I was getting off the bus, Mr. Avery said, "Seely, your pa gave you real good advice when he told you not to speak of Morton Chally. You mustn't ever repeat the things I say to you concerning him, either."

"I won't, Mr. Avery," I promised. Then I added, "And don't you say anything either."

I got home a few minutes before Robert. Mom was in the kitchen making an effort to get supper and trying to give the impression that everything was all right. She turned from the stove, as I closed the door, a questioning look on her face.

"Seely," she said. "I thought you'd be Robert. He's not home yet."

"He'll be here soon," I told her. "He was going to stop by and see Nellie and Mr. Paully on the way home from school."

"He shouldn't do that without first asking me," Mom said. "He's not old enough to do as he pleases."

"He asked, and I told him he could," I said, and went on to the front room.

I put the few pieces of wood that were in the woodbox on the smoldering remains of the fire in the heating stove and brought a huge chunk from the woodlot to lay on top of the blazing wood. The water bucket in the kitchen was empty, so I took it to the pump on the back porch to get water for the night.

Robert was coming across the yard, his head down, and dragging his feet. "Hurry up, Robert," I called to him. "Mom has supper ready, and we're waiting for you."

His head came up, and he smiled all over. "Mom's up?" he asked, disbelieving. "Oh boy!" And he ran the rest of the way to the house.

A moment later when I took the water inside, Robert had his arms around Mom's waist, his head snuggled close to her breast. Mom was smiling and smoothing his hair tenderly.

I hoped that this would be the turning point for Mom. She seemed so much better that for a few days I was sure it would be. But, before long, she was right back to spending the day in her bed or the rocking chair. Robert and I were once again trying to manage on our own.

This was dawdling-along-the-road weather, the kind that only comes in early April and doesn't last. So I was dawdling while I could. It had rained the night before, making the dirt road soft and muddy, so I'd had to wear my boots to school today. Now, on the way home, I waded into the weeds along the edge of the road and on the high banks, looking for signs of spring flowers. The new grass was showing green beneath the matted-down brown weeds, but I guess it was still too early for flowers. I didn't find any.

When I went through the gate at home, I saw Robert at the chopping block in the woodlot. He had the heavy double-bladed axe raised above his head, ready to bring it down on a chunk of wood. He glanced up and saw me as he brought the axe downward, and he missed the chopping block. The blade seemed to be buried in his foot; pinning him to the ground.

I screamed and started running toward him. At the same time, I heard Mom scream his name from the back porch.

I got to Robert just a moment before Mom did. Just time enough to pull the axe from his boot and throw it aside. He was crying so hard, I knew he must be nearly dying from the pain, yet I was afraid to take off his boot. Afraid of what I would find inside it.

Mom held Robert in her arms and I unbuckled his boot, pulling it gently from his foot. The axe had gone through the toe of his boot and completely missed his shoe. Robert's foot hadn't been touched.

"Hush your bawling," I said. "You're not hurt." In my relief at finding him unharmed, I had spoken sharply to him.

"I've ruined my good boots that Dad gave me," Robert cried.

Mom had her arms around him, still babying him. "Thank God," she said. "Rob bought those boots way too big to start with. If they had fit your shoes . . ." She shuddered and didn't finish. Then to Robert, "Don't cry, honey. We'll get new boots for you before you need them next year."

Not a word to him, I thought, about his having no business handling Dad's axe. And he should be told. He might not be so lucky the next time.

The box of food stuff from the county welfare was

sitting in the middle of the kitchen table. Probably where Aunt Fanny Phillips had put it, when she brought it in. It didn't look as if it had been touched or any effort made to put the stuff away.

Mom went to the porch to get water, and I started emptying the box of groceries. Robert came and leaned on the table, watching me.

"Don't be mad at me, Seely," he said, finally. "Before long, I'll be able to cut all the wood for you."

I said, "Robert, as soon as you stand taller than the axe handle, you can cut wood and split logs. But until then, you leave that axe alone."

"Seely, you don't have to be so harsh with Robert," Mom said. "He was just trying to help."

I set a can of corned beef down hard on the shelf and turned to get another can from the box. "He'll help the most," I mumbled, "by staying all in one piece till he's grown," and went on stacking cans on the shelf.

In the very bottom of the welfare box, I found dozens of packages of garden seeds. They hadn't sent just corn, beans, and pumpkin seeds this time, but there was an assortment of seeds for every vegetable that can be grown in a garden. They had even included seeds for zinias, marigolds, and nasturtiums for a small patch of flowers.

"Mom, look at these," I said, scattering the bright packets of seeds on the table. "With this many seeds you can have the biggest and best garden in the county this year."

Mom barely glanced at the garden seeds. "Clear that

stuff off the table, Seely, and set the places for supper," she said. "I don't know as I want to bother with a garden this summer," she added, and turned away.

I thought that she would be pleased to see the seeds they had provided for a garden. Mom had always liked working with plants and watching green things grow. Even last year, with the scant choice of seeds she'd had at hand and the few plants that Aunt Fanny had brought her to set out in the garden, Mom had grown vegetables enough for use on the table and some left over to can and put up for winter.

As I gathered up the colorful packages of vegetable and flower seeds from the table, I heard Mom mutter, "Last year's seed. I wouldn't waste my time." But I put the seeds on the top shelf of the cabinet, where she couldn't miss seeing them; in case she changed her mind. Then I set the table for supper.

Mom called, "Seely, get up!" My feet hit the floor running. I was halfway to the bedrom door, when she said, "It's six o'clock."

I stopped and waited for my heart to quit pounding. When I had heard her call me, I'd expected to hear that the house was on fire, or that we'd been hit by a tornado. Mom was as fearful of one as she was of the other.

"Seely?"

"I'm up," I answered.

Robert sat up in bed, rubbing his eyes, and yawning. "Seely, what's the matter?"

"Nothing is wrong, Robert," I said. "Mom is calling us to breakfast. And it's time to get ready for school."

He threw back the covers to get out of bed, and I left the room. I wanted to see if Mom really was getting breakfast. For more than a month now, Robert and I had been making our own breakfast, such as it was, and leaving for school without ever laying eyes on Mom.

"Seely, you're going to miss your bus," Mom said. "You are not even dressed yet."

She was dressed and her dark auburn hair smooth and neat in a roll on the back of her head. She turned from the stove, put her hands on her hips, and just looked at me. "You're a sight," she said, and smiled.

I hadn't touched Mom, or even come close to her, since Dad died. She hadn't seemed to want me near her. But this morning, with her smile as bright and welcome as the sun coming through the kitchen windows, I ran to put my arms around her.

"I'll be ready in a minute," I told her, and quickly left the room.

I didn't mind the long walk to the bus stop this morning, to catch the school bus. It seemed like having Mom standing in the door, smiling and waving to Robert and me as we left the house, made all the difference in the world in how I felt about everything.

Where our dirt lane met the gravel road, Mr. Avery was waiting patiently in his bus for me. I threw up my hand in a friendly wave, then ran and skipped the rest of the way to the bus.

"You keep on skipping your feet like that," Mr. Avery said, as I took my usual seat behind him, "and your shoe sole will fall off again."

"But it's too pretty a day just to walk," I said. "The air is so light, I think I could skip all the way to school and never touch the ground."

Mr. Avery didn't argue it. He had the window rolled down beside him, and the soft April breeze touched my face then lifted my hair gently off my neck and shoulders, like loving fingers brushing it away. I wished that we could go all the way to school like this. Not stopping for anyone else or having anything break into this morning.

"How's your ma feeling, Seely?" Mr. Avery asked softly. "Is she getting along all right?"

We had passed the Williams place and I hadn't even noticed. Porter Hollow, and the next stop, was just around the bend in the road.

I said, "Mom is fine, Mr. Avery." I smiled to myself. I could almost feel the warmth of that moment earlier this morning when Mom had smiled on me. "Mom's fine," I repeated softly.

Mr. Avery nodded his head and looked at me in the rearview mirror. "I figured as much," he said, when he caught my eye.

Mom semed more like herself every day, and she made no objection when I said that I was taking Robert to Aunt Fanny's to get his hair trimmed that Saturday. We asked her to go along, but she wouldn't. "I have things to do here at home," was her excuse. But I couldn't see anything that couldn't wait until we got back from Jubilee.

"Did your mother find the garden seeds that I put in the welfare box this week?" Aunt Fanny asked as she stacked books under Robert so she wouldn't have to bend to clip his hair. "I figured a few packets of seed would start her to thinking of a garden, and she wouldn't have so much time to brood about . . . other things," she added.

"Mom didn't know that you sent them," I replied. "She thought the welfare was sending last year's seeds to those on relief, and she said that old seed wouldn't sprout. No use wasting her time to make a garden, she says, so she's not going to use them," I added.

"We'll see whether or not she puts out a garden," Aunt Fanny said, snipping furiously at Robert's hair. "I'll send a man to work up the ground myself, and we'll sow them seeds. You kids are big enough to tend a garden, and you'll need the vegetables to live on this summer. Not to mention the canned stuff to be put by for next winter's needs."

I didn't mention to Mom what Aunt Fanny had said about a garden. Time enough to talk about that after the ground was plowed and worked down, ready to receive the seeds. And Robert didn't say anything either, though I kept expecting him to repeat every word that Aunt Fanny had said to us.

I don't know how she did it, but the next time she went to the welfare office to get our relief box, Aunt Fanny got Mom to go along with her. While they were away from the house, the garden was plowed, harrowed, and the clods dragged down until the garden was ready to be laid out in rows and seeded. Aunt Fanny stayed at the house with Mom until I got home from school, then she got in her car and went home.

"Fanny Phillips takes a lot for granted," Mom said, as soon as Aunt Fanny had gone. "One of these days she's going to overstep herself, and someone will put her in her place."

I went to the table and started looking in the cardboard welfare box to see what they had sent us this week, hoping that I would find something different. But it was the same old thing. Macaroni, canned tomatoes, canned corned beef, lard, sugar, and flour. There was a paper tray of peanut butter and a box of white margarine, with a little tablet of orange coloring, and a bucket of Karo syrup on top of everything else. I took the peanut butter and started to scrape it into a fruit jar, so I could cap it and keep it from drying out. Welfare must have got peanut butter by the bulk and ladled it out to the people on relief by the pound, putting it in the cheapest container they could find.

Mom said, "Seely, are you listening to me? Did you have a hand in getting that garden worked down?"

I screwed the lid tight on the peanut butter and reached for the margarine. It would have to be mixed before we could use it.

"Aunt Fanny did say something about a garden while she was cutting Robert's hair," I said, stalling for time, while I thought of a way to tell her what Aunt Fanny had said and still keep Mom in good humor. "I told her that you weren't thinking of a garden this year, but she said that Robert and I would be able to tend a garden."

"There's more to raising a garden than just dropping in the seeds," Mom said. "You can't do it alone, and Robert's too little to be of any help to you."

"Robert is nearly as old as Jamie was when we used to work the garden together," I said quietly. "He will do his share and then some."

I broke the little orange capsule into the white margarine, and started stirring it with a fork. Mom stood and watched me for a moment. Then she said, "I could mark off the rows for you, if I had a ball of twine and some stakes to use to mark the end of the row."

I looked out the window. The sun hadn't gone behind the hills yet. "There's still time for Robert to cut some branches with his pocket knife and whittle the stakes before dark. And I'll bring a roll of string home from the store, after school tomorrow evening. It won't take long with all three of us working at it," I added.

Mom went to the cabinet and got the garden seeds. Then she sat down at the table and started sorting through them. I called Robert from the other room and told him what we needed of him. "Cut oak or walnut limbs, Robert," I said. "Branches bigger than a pencil, but no larger than a man's thumb. And always hack away from yourself," I cautioned him. "You'd be no help if you cut off a finger."

157

Robert smiled at me, slapped the pocket where he carried his knife, and ran out of the house, headed straight for the woods on the other side of the meadow. About an hour later, he came back with a bundle of neatly trimmed branches, ready to be cut to the length Mom wanted for row markers.

The next afternoon when I got home from school, Mom and Nellie and Aunt Fanny were stepping off the rows and setting the stakes. Robert was standing off to one side of the garden with his hands in his pockets and his chin on his chest. "I thought it was supposed to be our garden," he muttered, when I asked what was the matter, "but they won't let me do anything."

"Never mind," I said. "As soon as they get the string tied in a straight line, you can help me plant the seed."

Robert brightened up at once. "I can?" he asked. Then his face dropped and he said, "Seely, how do you plant a seed?"

I smiled at him and started to put my arm around him, but he moved out of my reach. I let my hand drop and answered Robert as if he was as old as I was, or very nearly.

"I'll show you," I said. "You'll have the important part to do, digging the holes and making sure they are two feet apart and in a straight line with the string. I'll follow you, dropping seeds and covering them up. We won't get it done in one day," I added. "Or even two. It will more than likely take us all week, working every evening after school."

158

"That's all right," Robert said. "Just as long as I get to do my part in the garden, and I don't get left out of it."

Aunt Fanny gave Robert a ride home from school every day that week, stopping to pick up Nellie on the way, and we worked in the garden until Mom called us to supper. Nellie and Aunt Fanny made a show of checking the rows to see that Robert dug the holes deep enough and that I had hilled up the beans the way I should.

One evening, Aunt Fanny brought a sack of potatoes that had gone to seed: all eyes and long sprouts growing out of them. She said they weren't good for nothing. Probably wouldn't even grow. But we quartered them and put them in the ground anyway. When we were all finished with the planting, Robert stood back and looked at the garden as if he expected to see plants popping up along the rows and seemed disappointed not to.

"Come a good rain, Robert," Nellie said, "and you'll have more plants and weeds than you know what to do with."

chapter sixteen

M r. Avery stopped the bus, and Peedle Porter laughed as he slipped by Annabel Grewe and into the seat beside me.

"All right for you, Peedle," Annabel said. She smacked him lightly on the back, then took the seat behind us.

The oldest Knight boy slid into the seat beside Annabel. "Annie, you're always threatening to write Peedle, yet I never see Peedle getting any letters."

"Roy, don't call me Annie! I've told you before that I don't like it," Annabel said.

I turned and looked behind me. As far as I could recall, I had never heard Annabel speak to one of the Knight boys. They walked home together, taking the same path over the hill, yet they had never seemed like friends. Just people going the same way, at the same time.

"Why don't you go sit with your brothers?" Annabel said.

Roy Knight grinned at her, then slid down in the seat, bracing his long legs against the back of Peedle's seat to make himself comfortable. "I like it here, where I'm at, Annie," he said.

Annabel flounced away from him, as far as she could get in such close quarters. When she saw me watching, she rolled her eyes and said, "I know, Seely. It's the cross I have to bear for being so irresistible to growing boys."

Roy Knight gave a hearty burst of laughter. Annabel ignored him and went on talking to me.

Peedle Porter turned in his seat to explain something to Roy Knight.

"It's spelled different," Peedle said.

"What's spelt differently, Peedle?" Roy had his eyes closed, and he didn't open them to answer Peedle.

"What Annabel always say to me," Peedle said. "She's not talking about write, like a letter. She means that one day she will get even with me," he explained patiently.

Roy Knight opened his eyes and sat up straight in his seat. "The day that Annie is even with you," he said, his face dead serious, "is the day I'm waiting for, Peedle."

"Idiots!" Annabel said. "Nothing but idiots!" She gave an exaggerated sigh, and we all laughed, Peedle laughing harder than anyone else.

School wouldn't be out for more than five weeks—at the end of the first week of June—yet there seemed to be a lighthearted liveliness about everyone today, giving the feeling that tomorrow was the last day of school.

And the festive feeling lasted right up to the time everyone stepped off the bus to go home that evening.

Aunt Fanny Phillips was at our house when I got home. There was a big box on the back seat of her car, and when I met her coming out our back door, she had a smaller box in her hands.

She seemed taken back, abashed, at meeting me. Then she got hold of herself and smiled at me.

"The church at Shiloh is having a bazaar," she said. "Zel and me have been doing her spring housecleaning, to get something to donate to it." Aunt Fanny kind of laughed. "Charity is supposed to start at home," she said, "and your mother and me didn't want to leave ours to the very last."

She took the box to her car, and I went on into the house. There seemed to be a bareness, like something wasn't in its usual place, but I couldn't name anything that was missing from the house. Aunt Fanny came back inside to tell Mom that she would be over again in the morning. "I can think of quite a few others that we should see for donation," she said, as she was leaving.

I started to my bedroom to hang up my jacket. The door to the upstairs was open, and the whole house seemed lighter. I stopped and just looked.

"We took the newspapers off the upstairs windows," Mom said, from close behind me. "There was all that stuff up there that Linzy Meaders left when she went away, so we got it sorted and boxed it all for the church sale. Linzy will never want it," Mom added, "and maybe someone else can use it."

Robert came clattering down the stairs like a small elephant, just freed from captivity. "Seely, we could move our beds upstairs now," he said. "If you want to. There's nothing up there now, except cleanness."

Mom said, "You'll do no such thing. I want you where I can lay hands on you. If need be," she added.

Robert looked puzzled. I think he must have felt the same as I did, but he could no more put a name to it than I could. It wasn't just the clean freshness of the house. Mom was acting different too. Like Mom again.

It seemed to me that Mom had started coming to her senses the minute she had seen that axe coming down straight for Robert's foot the other evening. Up to then, it had been as though she'd been asleep for a month, and it had taken the sight of Robert being threatened with harm to wake her up. Now she was more like her old self again. Her brown eyes were still sad and sober, but her face didn't have that angry look about it any longer. It seemed almost peaceful.

We were eating supper when I realized what it was that I'd missed seeing in the kitchen. No matter where we lived, I had always seen it hanging on a hook on the kitchen door.

"Dad's sheepskin coat is gone!" I left the table to touch the spot where it had always hung. The door was bare and empty.

Mom said, "Seely, come to the table and finish your supper. Aunt Fanny took the coat and cap for the church bazaar."

"But that was Dad's good sheepskin coat," I said, and

163

started to cry. As long as his coat hung on the back of the door, I didn't feel like he was really gone. A man doesn't go away and leave his one good coat.

Mom came to me and took me in her arms, holding me close and letting me cry out all the tears that I hadn't shed earlier.

When at last I'd stopped my crying and I was ready to listen to reason, Mom sat with Robert and me and talked to us as she had never done before.

"Yesterday, when Aunt Fanny brought the county food stuff," Mom began, "she made me sit down and listen to her. I didn't want to hear what she had to say," Mom said. "But she made me see the folly of holding on to Rob's things. Aunt Fanny told me that as long as I kept Rob's coat and cap in plain sight, a constant reminder of him, the harder it would be to admit he was gone, to give him up and go on living without him."

Mom stopped speaking and looked at her hands, folded together on the table in front of her. "I didn't want to go on living without him," she said, her voice low, "but I had no choice, the way I see it."

Robert and I didn't say anything. Mom sat there, turning the wide wedding band round and round on her finger. Finally, she said, "Your daddy didn't have much. I gave it all away, except his pipe. I've kept that. It's in the trunk where I have all my other keepsakes."

"And you kept nothing else of Dad's?" I asked.

Mom looked at me, her eyes soft and gentle, then reached to draw Robert close to her. "Seely, I have you and your brother. What other remembrance would I ever need of your daddy?"

After supper, Robert went to the garden to see if the plants had sprouted through the ground, then came back to the house to report to Mom and me. "I think you buried the seeds too deep," he said to me. "There's not a sign of green anywhere in the garden."

He went to his room to study, and Mom and I did the dishes. It seemed like now that Mom had started talking about Dad, she couldn't stop. Her voice went on and on, recounting the things Dad had said and done. It was good to be able to say his name and to recall his never-flagging hope that there would be better days ahead for us all.

"Dad always said a body made his own lot," I said, thinking aloud.

"Aunt Fanny said much the same thing, when I was fussing about being on relief," Mom said. "She seems to think if I applied myself, I could make a living right here at home. I could get off welfare."

I was curious to know what Aunt Fanny had in mind, and wondered if she had told Mom. "Did she say how you could do that?" I asked.

"Why," Mom said, "she's got the notion that I could bake pies and sell them to the restaurants in Oolitic or Bedford. Fanny says that a homemade pie is a treat to the city folk, and they're not shy about paying for it, either."

While Mom was talking, I figured in my head about how much it would cost to make a pie and what she

165

would have to ask for one to make a profit. We had canned peaches, pumpkin, and blackberries for filling, and the rhubarb was almost ready to use. The early June apples would be coming on before she ran out of the stuff on hand. We were blessed with sugar, flour, and lard. Every week the welfare sent a new supply, and we hadn't used a third of it.

Mom looked at me anxiously. "Well, Seely," she said. "Do you think we could make a living baking for the city folks?"

It made me feel proud that Mom would discuss this with me and ask my opinion for my thoughts on the matter, and I didn't want to discourage her. But there was a distance of quite a few miles between our house and the restaurants in Oolitic.

"How would you ever get the pies to town, once they were baked?" I asked.

"Aunt Fanny thought of that," Mom said. "She talked like she might be willing to take me to Oolitic, should I decide to do it." Mom glanced around the room, making sure everything was taken care of. "But I couldn't allow her to drive me there for nothing," she added.

She picked up the oil lamp to light our way to the front room and then to bed. The lamp was still burning in Mom's bedroom when I went to sleep.

Mom was dressed and ready and waiting for Aunt Fanny when Robert and I left for school the next morning. Robert asked her where she was going, and Mom told him that she had promised to go scavenging with

166

Aunt Fanny today, searching for salvageable stuff for the church bazaar.

"But I have some things of my own that I want to see about today," she said, "and I may not be here when you get home this evening. Just go ahead and do your chores, and don't worry about me. I'll be home before dark," she added, with a smile.

Robert and I both smiled back. That was what she always told us when we were out in the evening, "Be sure you get home before dark, so I won't worry." And now she was promising us the same.

I wondered if she had decided to bake the pies and try her hand at selling them. That was probably one of the things she wanted to look into today, I thought. Maybe talk to restaurant owners and find out whether or not they would be interested in buying her pies.

I couldn't picture Mom going up to strangers and asking them to buy her pies. Yet, I couldn't see her continuing to stay on the county welfare rolls either. Not if there was any way open to her to help herself.

Mr. Avery gave me his customary greeting as I got on the bus, but there seemed to be an undercurrent of excitement in his voice, like a small boy with a big secret, just waiting to find someone to tell it to. Now he had found someone, and it didn't take him long to tell me.

Before we had rounded the bend at the foot of the hill, Mr. Avery said, "Seely, do you recollect me saying that I would keep you posted should I hear any word of Morton Chally?"

He tilted his head back, and his eyes sought mine in the rearview mirror. I nodded my head yes, I remembered. "Has he come back to the Williams place?" I asked.

"I guess you might say that he tried to," Mr. Avery replied. And he didn't say anything more for quite a ways down the road.

Then he said, "You won't hear a word out of the Knight boys about this. They've got their orders to keep quiet from old man Knight, and the boys know better than to go against their pa's word. He's strict but fair," Mr. Avery added, "and tougher than whang leather."

"But what about Morton Chally?" I asked him.

I think if Mr. Avery had still been chewing tobacco, he would have spit. "I'm getting to him, Seely," he said, and rubbed his mouth with his hand, as if he had.

"Chally was cutting across the hills last night, passed the Knights' house, aiming to come to the Williams place from the back part of the farm. In the darkness," Mr. Avery said, "Chally stumbled into the Knights' hog pen, into the nest where one of the old sows had her litter of pigs. That sow nearly ripped Morton Chally to bits before his screams were heard inside the Knight house. The old man and the boys got him out of the hog pen and sent for the hearse. They thought he was done for," Mr. Avery added. "But I was talking to the undertaker, and he said that Chally wasn't at his place. He was at the clinic in Bedford."

I felt sick. Just the thought of a man being torn apart

by an angry hog turned my stomach. "Oh," I said. "That's awful!"

"Yes, it is," Mr. Avery agreed. "But when a sow with a litter of pigs is threatened, she can be mighty vicious. You might say," he added quietly, "almost as mean and vicious as Morton Chally."

"Mr. Avery, I'm not feeling sorry for the man," I said. "I just think it's awful."

Mr. Avery shook his head and didn't reply.

When we passed the Williams place, he motioned toward the farm. "I hear that Onalee is trying to get rid of the place," he said. "But no one around here seems to want it. They say there's a jinx on it."

I said that I didn't know whether the farm had a jinx on it or not, but it sure hadn't brought a lot of good luck to Onalee Chally. "Or for that matter," I said, "Russell Williams and his dad weren't blessed with luck either."

Mr. Avery was right about the Knight boys not having anything to say concerning what had happened at their house the night before. They looked kind of peaked, but they got on the bus and went straight to the back row of seats. Roy Knight didn't even stop to tease Annabel Grewe this morning.

chapter seventeen

Annabel and Roxie and
I sat in the school bus to eat our lunch. Then we went
into the Averys' store to look around. Not one of us had
a nickel to our name. We couldn't have bought a penny
stick of candy. But Mrs. Avery smiled when she saw us
walk in and came from behind the counter to speak to us.

Mrs. Avery asked about our friend Ogretta Roberts
the first thing. She seemed pleased and happy to know
that Gretta was home from the hospital. "But she still
has to go back there for treatment," Annabel told her.
"And use the crutches to get around the house."

"Ogretta has kept up on her lessons," Annabel said,
when Mrs. Avery lamented the time she had lost in
school. "She won't be held back," she added, "and we'll
all four be juniors together next year."

Mrs. Avery smiled. "And how do you all aim to
spend your summer?" she asked.

We looked at each other, then at Mrs. Avery. I doubt that any one of us had given a thought to what we'd do when school was out until this very minute.

Roxie shrugged her shoulders. "Same as last summer, I guess," she said, with a lopsided grin. "I'll help my brothers in the fields all week, then take care of the neighbor's kids on Saturday."

Annabel said that she was going to stay with her widowed aunt in Louisville again this summer and take care of her kids. "She can work all right while the kids are in school," Annabel said, "but they're not old enough to be left alone when school is out."

Roxie looked at Annabel enviously and said, "I wish I could go, too!"

I didn't say anything. I hadn't even thought as far ahead as summer. Taking care of each day as it came along had been almost more than I could handle.

Mrs. Avery said, "What about you, Seely? What are you going to do when school is out?"

"I guess I'll go on doing the same as I do now," I replied. "Only then, I'll have all week to do it in."

The three minute bell rang at the schoolhouse, and we three girls turned to leave the store. Mrs. Avery put her hand on my arm. "Seely," she said in a low voice, "come and talk to me later." I replied that I would and hurried after Annabel and Roxie.

I should have stayed at home. Not even come to school today, I thought, as Roxie Treadwell and I waited for Mr. Drayer in his office. Better still, I should have kept out of it. Roxie hadn't asked for my help, I told myself. But I had been with her.

We had been on our way to the Home Economics class. Halfway down the stairs, Jummy Lewis grabbed Roxie from behind and pushed himself against her. "Meet me in the furnace room," he said to her. "Baby, I can make Charlie look like a piker."

Roxie cried out and tried to elbow him away. But Jummy just laughed and squeezed her tighter. When Roxie cried out again, I raised the books I held in my hand and brought them down hard on Jummy Lewis's head, just like bringing the axe down on a chunk of wood.

Jummy's arms dropped from around Roxie. He sat down on the steps with a stunned look on his face and slid the rest of the way down stairs.

There had been a lot of confusion after that, and Roxie and I had been sent to the principal's office to be reprimanded for our behavior.

"It's not fair!" I moved to the window, to stand next to Roxie. "Jummy Lewis started the trouble, but we're the ones who are getting blamed for it."

Roxie turned from staring out the window, her dark eyes moist. "I'll probably get expelled from school," she said. "I've missed so many days, and that mess with Charlie Buskirk; Mr. Drayer is not going to listen to a thing I say," she added.

"But I'm the one who knocked Jummy Lewis down the stairs," I said. "And I'll tell Mr. Drayer so. It wasn't your fault that he was picking on you. You didn't do anything."

"It won't do any good," Roxie said, defeated before we ever started.

Mr. Drayer came in then. He just stood and looked at us, shaking his head. "What am I going to do with you two girls?" he said.

I raised my head, ready to face the music. And I knew beforehand, from the looks of him, that it would be a tune I didn't like. Roxie and I waited for the other to speak, or for Mr. Drayer to go on.

"I've heard three versions of how you knocked Jummy Lewis down the stairs," Mr. Drayer said, looking at me. "Seely, suppose you tell me now how you did it."

I told him what had happened. How Jummy Lewis had held Roxie and wouldn't let her go. But I didn't tell him what Jummy had said to Roxie. "Roxie cried out and tried to get away from him," I said. "I thought Jummy was hurting her, so I hit him with my books. He slid down the stairs," I finished.

Mr. Drayer walked back and forth in front of us, his hands clasped together behind his back and his face turned away.

"Seely, how many times have you been in here, and I've had to speak to you about fighting with the other kids?"

My lower lip held out stubbornly beneath the upper lip, I said, "I don't know."

He did some more pacing up and down. Counting the

times, I thought. But when he spoke, he was off on another tangent.

"You've got to learn to get along with the other students," he said. "Conform. Follow their lead and do as they do and you won't have this trouble all the time."

"No," I said, shaking my head. "I won't do that."

As Mr. Drayer stopped in front of me, his face set and stern, Roxie stepped closer to me. Her dark eyes were frightened, pleading with me to hold my tongue and not antagonize him further.

He seemed to speak to me through his clenched teeth, as if he was afraid he'd scream at me if he opened his mouth. "Seely, would you be so kind as to give me one good reason why you can't do as I say?"

"I just can't," I said. Then thinking that I might as well be hung for a sheep as a goat, I went on. "Mom would skin me alive if she ever heard of me doing the things some of them do," I said. "They're like a flock of dumb chickens, poking fun at us because we're poor and pecking away at the ones who were born different from them. As if it makes them richer and smarter to pick on us. That's what they do," I added stubbornly, "and that is what you are asking me to do. And I won't do it."

Mr. Drayer stepped to within an arm's reach of me. "You are incorrigible," he said. "From what you've told me yourself, Jummy Lewis wasn't bothering you. Yet you struck him."

"He was bothering Roxie. And she's my friend."

He looked at me for a long time, and I looked right back. Finally, he let his breath out in a long whoosh and

174

turned away. "You can go now," Mr. Drayer said. "But I'm going to talk to your parents about this, later."

I walked out of the principal's office and went straight out the front door of the schoolhouse. Roxie hesitated when we left the office, then she lifted her chin, squared her shoulders, and went along with me.

"Where are we going, Seely?" Roxie was hurrying to keep up with me.

"I don't know," I said. "But I know I'm not going back in there." I knew I had to go to school until I was sixteen, so I added, "For the rest of the day." And kept on walking.

Roxie and I sat in Mr. Avery's school bus for the rest of the day. Sometimes talking, but most of the time thinking and not saying a word.

I asked Roxie if she would be in trouble at home when Mr. Drayer called her dad about today. "Mr. Drayer is going to be madder than ever when he finds out we skipped school," I said. "No telling what he's apt to say to your dad."

Roxie kind of smiled and scuffed the toes of her shoes on the floorboards. "It doesn't matter what the principal tells him," Roxie said. "Dad works on the WPA and he's so beat when he gets home at night that he doesn't want to hear what happened here at school." She grinned at me. "He's not apt to take a day off from work to come here and argue with the teacher," she said. "Dad will tell Mr. Drayer that he does his work, and the teachers should do theirs. And that will be the end of it," Roxie added.

"I wish I could say it doesn't matter," I said, "but it does. Mom is going to be upset that I made trouble at school. And I didn't want to do anything to upset her now. She's been feeling so good lately," I added, my voice low.

We sat and worried quietly about the trouble we had gotten ourselves into. How quickly it had started, and how far it had spread in so little time. Everything we do seems to affect someone else, I thought. We're not just a single person, answerable only to ourselves, but an extension of a lot of other people.

"Who would've thought that hitting Jummy Lewis over the head could end up by hurting Mom," I said.

For a moment Roxie just looked at me. Then she said, "Who would've thought that Charlie Buskirk would blab about the furnace room to Jummy Lewis? And it had to be Charlie who told him," she added. "None of the rest of us will speak to the little creep."

I had nothing to say to that so we sat without talking. Each of us was thinking about our own predicament.

After a while, Roxie said, "It's not easy having to grow up and go to school at the same time."

And I replied, "No, it's not."

Mr. Avery didn't seem to be a bit surprised to find Roxie and me sitting in the school bus. He drove us back to school. Then Roxie got out and ran over to get on the Guthrie school bus.

While we were waiting for school to let out and the

other kids to get there, Mr. Avery asked, "You girls been skipping school today?"

"Just for a while," I said. Then I told him what had happened and why I had walked out of school. "I'll be in for it tomorrow," I told him. "But I just couldn't face anyone for a while."

The bell rang, dismissing school, and I went stiff all over. Now, I'd have to face the other kids and listen to their questions.

Mr. Avery cleared his throat to get my attention. I raised my head and looked at him.

"Seely, the fuss will be forgotten sooner if you don't dwell on it," he said gently. "I know that kids are nosey, and generally they don't care who they hurt with their questions. They'll want to hear all about your trouble, but just remember, the less said about it, the better it will be."

No one said anything until Jummy Lewis came aboard. Then someone from the rear of the bus called, "Hey, Jummy. Watch your step! Young Miss Dempsey is sitting in the first seat."

Everyone laughed, and snickers followed Jummy Lewis as he swaggered down the aisle. Mr. Avery watched him in the rearview mirror, making sure that Jummy didn't start anything. But he seemed properly cowed for once. He took the first empty seat he came to, without even looking to see who he was sitting with.

Annabel Grewe nudged me and smiled. "It sounds like Jummy Lewis is to be the butt of their jokes tonight," she said, her voice low. "You made him look like such a silly ass today that now he doesn't frighten anyone."

When Mr. Avery thought that the remarks had gone on too long, he stood up and faced the rear of the bus. "All right," he said. "Stop that foolishness, or you'll all walk home. No sense running something in the ground," he muttered, as he took his seat and headed the bus toward home.

chapter eighteen

Annabel, Peedle, and the Knight boys had left the bus at the last stop, and Mr. Avery and myself were the only ones on the bus. Now I could ask him what I had in mind, without feeling too stupid. It had been bothering me all afternoon, and I didn't want to wait till I got to school tomorrow to find out.

"Mr. Avery," I said, "what does it mean to be incorrigible?"

He glanced at me in the mirror, then looked quickly back to the road. "That's a pretty big word, Seely. Where did you hear it?"

"The principal, Mr. Drayer, he said I was incorrigible," I answered. "I was going to look it up in the dictionary, but he made me so mad that I forgot and walked out of school. We don't have a dictionary at home," I explained.

"That's just as well," Mr. Avery said, using his mirror to look at me again. "You could get the wrong notion about yourself, reading it in a book, and the word doesn't fit you, Seely. Put it out of your mind and forget it," he added.

"But, Mr. Avery, I ought to know what it means," I said, "in case Mr. Drayer really tells Mom, like he says he's going to do."

Mr. Avery moved uncomfortably in his seat, coughed, and rubbed his mouth with the back of his hand. I could tell he didn't want to pursue this any farther, but since I had asked him, he felt honor bound to answer.

"Your ma won't listen to no such thing," Mr. Avery said, indignation in every word. "She knows you're not a wild one that can't be corrected or made to behave. Not even the school principal could make her believe that," he muttered under his breath.

"I hope you're right," I said. I didn't feel as confident about it as he did.

I still wasn't sure what was meant by incorrigible. But it sounded like a big word for what Mom had been telling me ever since I'd been old enough to walk and talk. And even though I hadn't heard it for some time now, I wasn't likely to forget it. "Seely," Mom used to say, "you don't listen, or pay any attention to a word I tell you."

I was afraid that when Dr. Drayer sent his letter of

180

complaint about me to Mom, it would remind her, and she would remember what she used to tell me.

I wished that the school principal was more like Mr. Avery. Someone who understood that you couldn't help but make mistakes. Not if you did what you thought you should. At the time, it seemed to be the right thing to do, even though it turned out to be the wrong thing later on. Mr. Avery would understand that you can't always be right about everything.

The bus stopped at our lane, and halfway down the steps I turned to tell Mr. Avery goodbye. Instead, I heard myself saying," I wish everybody in the world was like you, Mr. Avery. Then I wouldn't have a thing to worry about."

My words surprised both of us, but Mr. Avery got over his surprise at once. "See you tomorrow," he said. I ducked my head and jumped the rest of the way to the ground.

I ran across the road to the mailbox, hoping to find a letter from Julie, but the box was empty. We had one letter from Julie since she had gone back to school, after Dad's funeral. I didn't know if Mom had even answered it. I wrote letters to Julie all the time, telling her how things were here at home, but I never mailed them. I only wrote them to make myself feel better, not to worry her with our troubles. I knew that she couldn't do anything to help. And besides that, I didn't have the pennies to buy stamps to mail my letters.

A while back, I had even written a letter to Julie telling her that Mr. Avery and I were thinking to find a way to prove that Morton Chally had deliberately killed Russell Williams, just like he had destroyed Russell's mare and colt. But I had burned that letter. I would write her another one later, when the matter was settled and I knew the ending, and I would mail that one to her.

I had been so absorbed in my own problems this evening that I had forgotten to ask Mr. Avery if he had heard anything more about Chally. And he probably knew a lot, if I had just given him the chance to tell me. More than likely, I thought, as I neared the top of the ridge, he had been waiting for the other kids to leave the bus so he could tell me. But I had butted in with my question, and now I would have to wait until tomorrow morning to find out if Chally was living or dead.

I knew then that I didn't wish Morton Chally dead. I hadn't for a long time now. His death wouldn't bring Russell back or make Onalee's life any easier. It would just be another end to living and not accomplish a thing. I still wanted to see Chally punished, but not dead punished. That was too final. Perhaps they could just lock him away where he could never, ever harm anyone. Not ever again.

I was walking right in the middle of the road, and Aunt Fanny nearly ran over me as she drove out of our gate and onto the road. There was just time for me to see that Robert was in the car with her, as I leaped to one side, out of her way. I wondered where they were going in such a hurry, and I ran to the house to ask Mom.

"Fanny will be right back with Robert," Mom said,

before I could ask. "She's going to eat supper with us tonight."

It wasn't unusual for Aunt Fanny to eat at our house, but she hadn't for a long time now. When Dad had been working at Crowe, and we knew he wouldn't be home for supper, and Gus Tyson was tied up with work at the sawmill, Aunt Fanny would come to our house, bringing whatever she had on hand to eat, and we'd have supper together. She always said, "I'm going to wear out my welcome, coming here so often." But we had never tired of having her at our table.

She was going to be especially welcome tonight, I thought to myself. Mom wouldn't be nearly as apt to ask me about my day at school with Aunt Fanny here to talk to.

"Seely, wash your hands and set the places on the table," Mom said. "Fanny and Robert will be back in a minute."

I did as I was told, thinking all the while that as fast as Aunt Fanny drove that car, Mom was probably right about the time. And she didn't miss it much. By the time I had the table ready, Aunt Fanny and Robert were walking through the door.

Aunt Fanny put a pan of walnut pudding on the table, which she had brought to go with our biscuits and stew, and took a deep sniff of the air. "Zel," she said, "I don't know what you've got cooking in that skillet, but it sure smells good."

"Hobo stew," Mom told her. "It's a concoction I threw together in a pan the first night we ever camped out beside the road." She explained to Aunt Fanny how she made it with canned corned beef, onions, and potatoes, "and anything else that's handy," Mom said. "But I don't usually serve it to company."

Aunt Fanny laughed. "I'm not company, Zel. After all this time," she said, "I feel like I'm one of the family."

And she talked and acted like one of the family too. She and Mom didn't pay a lot of attention to Robert and me during the meal. They were busily recapping their day of gathering rummage for the church sale. Other than dishing up stew or passing the biscuits, when we asked, they ignored us.

Aunt Fanny seemed real pleased with the things they had gotten from the well-to-do people in Bedford. "We should realize a sizable sum," she said. "If the sale goes well."

Mom agreed with her, remarking that these people had thrown away better dresses than she wore for Sunday. "But I don't envy them," Mom said. "It would plague me no end to have so many dresses that I couldn't decide which one to wear."

As soon as we finished eating, Robert excused himself, saying he had homework to do. "I'm going to the front room," he said. "I can't hear myself think. Not with all the gabbing going on in here," he muttered, as he left the room.

I got up and cleared the table, taking everything but the coffee cups. I left them, so that Mom and Aunt Fanny could finish their coffee and talk, while I did the dishes. I probably wouldn't have paid any attention to what they were saying had Aunt Fanny not lowered her voice, as if she was giving away a secret that she didn't want me to hear.

"Zel, while you were asking for donations from the Buchers today," Aunt Fanny said," I went to see Pearl Fiscus. She works nights at the Bedford Clinic. And she was telling me that the hearse brought Morton Chally in there last night more dead than alive. He'd been nearly torn to pieces," she added, "by one of the Knights' old sows."

I stopped washing dishes and stood real still to listen.

"Chally chewed up by a hog!" Mom was horrified at the thought. "I've heard tell of sows that eat their young, if they are not separated, but I've never heard of one attacking a man. Did she say how it happened?" Mom asked.

Aunt Fanny lowered her voice even more, and I stepped closer so I could hear her.

"Pearl says there were some who thought Chally was trying to steal old man Knight's pigs, and I wouldn't put it past him," Aunt Fanny said. "But like I told Pearl, I figure Chally was sneaking back to the Williams place for some reason unbeknown to the rest of us, and in the dark he just stumbled into the pigpen."

"That's what Mr. Avery thinks too," I blurted out. "He told me that he figures Morton Chally accidentally fell into the sow's nest with the little pigs, and the old sow was trying to protect them."

Mom and Aunt Fanny both turned to look at me, and too late to do any good, I clapped my hand over my mouth and waited for them to rebuke me for interrupting them.

"Seely, since you've seen fit to stick your nose into our conversation," Mom said, "suppose you tell us what else the bus driver had to say about Morton Chally."

Mom's face was just as stern as her voice, warning me that she would brook no foolishness from me, and I'd better not try to sidestep her question. And I didn't.

"He didn't have a chance to tell me anything else," I answered. "The other kids started getting on the bus, and he doesn't talk to me about Chally when there's anyone else around."

Aunt Fanny sat forward in her chair, as if reaching to draw more information from me. "Surely, he mentioned it coming home tonight," she said. "Him having that store in town, and seeing folks all day, he must have heard something about it."

"No, he didn't mention it," I said, my head down, speaking to the floor. "And if he did hear anything, I didn't give him a chance to tell me."

I raised my eyes to Mom's face. "I did most of the talking after the other kids left the bus tonight," I told her.

Mom looked back at me for a long moment. "Seely, what are you trying to hide from me?"

I said, "I'm not trying to hide anything from you, Mom. I just didn't want to upset you."

"Upset me!" Mom raised her eyes toward heaven, as if asking for help to understand my reasoning. "What have you done now," she said, "that would upset me to know about?"

I looked at Aunt Fanny, sitting there with her eyes on me and her ears wide open, then I looked at Mom. I hadn't intended to tell Mom what happened at school in this manner. I had hoped to ease into it, to make it sound like a nothing-to-fret-about thing. But now I had no choice except to say it straight out and hope for her understanding.

"I hit Jummy Lewis over the head with my books," I said, "and knocked him down the steps. Mr. Drayer said that I was incorrigible and he's going to talk to you about it," I added quickly.

Mom opened her mouth to speak, but Aunt Fanny shook her head and motioned for Mom to wait. "Seely must have had good cause to hit that boy," she said quietly. "She wouldn't do a thing like that for no reason at all."

Then Aunt Fanny turned to me and nodded her head, meaning that I should go ahead and tell them why I had hit Jummy Lewis. Time was when Byron and I wouldn't have told Aunt Fanny anything. But she seemed more tolerant now. Tonight, I felt like she was on my side. She would see the sense in what I had done and not hold me to blame for it.

"Dad told me last fall that I wasn't to fight," I said. "He said that I was old enough now to talk my way out of trouble. But I guess I'm not really. I couldn't think of a thing to say to Jummy Lewis when he grabbed Roxie Treadwell."

187

I shifted from one foot to the other and looked at the floor. "He said some awful things to Roxie," I said, my voice low. "And she tried to get away from him, but she couldn't. When she cried out, like he was hurting her, I hit him over the head with my books."

I raised my head. Aunt Fanny was nodding her head, a satisfied expression on her face. But Mom seemed to be bridling a fierce anger and holding her tongue by a great effort.

"Zel, I thought as much," Aunt Fanny said. "Seely had no other course of action but to hit the boy. She couldn't let him hurt that girl."

Mom looked at me. "What did the principal have to say to this boy who started the trouble?"

"I don't think Mr. Drayer had talked to Jummy Lewis yet," I answered. "Anyhow, he hadn't when I left the schoolhouse."

"That's what I figured," Mom said, giving way to her anger. "He'll be let go without a word. And I dare say, his folks won't be bothered either." She nodded her head at Aunt Fanny, as if to say she was wise to these things. "That principal at the school is just picking on Seely."

"Mom, Mr. Drayer wasn't picking on me," I said. "He always talks to the kids whenever there's any trouble at school. He'll probably be talking to Roxie and me again tomorrow," I added. "Just as soon as he hears that we skipped school today."

"He needn't think he can walk roughshod over me and my kids, just because I'm a widow woman," Mom said, as if she hadn't heard a word I'd said. "I can tell him as well as the next one—" She stopped suddenly and gave me a hard, piercing look. "You skipped school? Left the schoolhouse without permission? Seely, what were you thinking about to do such a thing?"

"I guess I wasn't thinking," I said, my voice low. "I just wanted to get away from there."

"Seely, your willfulness will drive me to my grave," Mom said wearily. "You've got to learn that you can't do as you please. You do what you *have* to do first, *then* what you want. If it's allowed," she added.

Her shoulders slumped forward, and she lowered her head. "Go to your room, Seely," Mom said, waving her hand toward me, shooing me away from her. "I've had all I can stand of you for one night."

"Mom—" I began.

Her head came up, and her brown eyes caught me before I could go on. "I'll not tell you again," she said.

I left the room, but I heard her say to Aunt Fanny, "That girl tries my patience to no end, but she's not wild and unmanageable. And I won't have it said that she is."

Robert had left the lamp burning bright in the front room and gone on to bed. I turned the wick down low, then I went to bed. But it was a while before I went to sleep, or even tried to. There was a lot on my mind that puzzled me. Especially the way Mom had taken the news that Mr. Drayer wanted to talk to her about me. I hadn't thought that she would take my part against him.

For weeks and weeks now, I had been careful not to upset Mom or cause her any worry. And I hadn't wanted to upset her tonight. Yet it seemed like this was the best

189

thing I could've done for her. Aunt Fanny had gotten Mom out of the rocking chair and out of the house, and that was a start toward making her feel better. And now tonight, I had given Mom something to think on besides herself, a reason to exercise her right as a mother and start acting like one again.

After a while, I heard Aunt Fanny leave the house and the sound of the door bolted behind her. The light went out in the kitchen, and Mom's slow steps crossed the front room to turn out the light I'd left burning on the stand table. I turned over in bed and went to sleep.

chapter nineteen

I wasn't surprised the next morning when Miss Hendricks came to the study hall and told me that I was wanted in the principal's office. I'd been waiting ever since I got there for the summons. I knew Mr. Drayer wouldn't let the day go by without reprimanding me for playing hooky from school the day before.

As we walked out of the room together, Miss Hendricks had a bewildered look on her face, but she didn't say anything until we were nearly to the library.

"You're an intelligent girl, Seely," she said. "How do you always manage to undo your good grades with poor conduct reports?"

I said, "I don't know, Miss Hendricks. Seems like every way I turn, I bump into some kind of trouble."

She just shook her head, still puzzled.

At the door to the office, Miss Hendricks put her hand on my arm and said, "Try not to rub him the wrong way this morning." She smiled and formed an O with her thumb and forefinger. "Use a little diplomacy with him, Seely," she whispered and left me.

I opened the door without knocking and walked in. Then came a real surprise. Mom and Aunt Fanny Phillips were sitting at one side of Mr. Drayer's desk, and the air felt charged, as if sparks had just recently been flying through the room. I looked at the three of them, closed the door gently behind me, and remained standing just inside the door.

"Come in, Seely," Mr. Drayer said, motioning for me to come closer to his desk. "Now that I have met your mother, I can see where you get your spirit," he added dryly.

I stepped nearer to the desk and looked at Mom. She raised her head proudly and faced Mr. Drayer. "You don't see anything yet," she said. And I knew she had been here quite a while before I was ever sent for.

"You don't see that her father and me, we didn't raise our young ones to be victims," Mom said. "Nor to follow like sheep, without giving a thought to where it could lead. They've been taught to think and do for themselves," she added.

"I'll grant you," Mom went on, "Seely is too impulsive and outspoken for her own good, but incorrigible"—and here she came down hard on the word—"that she is not!"

I had never loved my mother as much as I did right then. She was holding up for me, taking my side against the school principal, and excusing my waywardness as if it was something to be proud of. I felt a stinging in my eyes, and I was afraid I was going to shame her by crying in front of them. I lowered my eyes and I wouldn't look at her.

"Hold your head up, Seely," Mom said. "You've done nothing to be ashamed of."

I raised my head and looked at Mr. Drayer. He kind of ducked his head, held up both hands, like he was surrendering under fire, and gave Mom a weak smile.

"Mrs. Robinson, perhaps in Seely's case," Mr. Drayer said, "that was too strong a word to use. And I apologize for my blunder." He leaned toward Mom and lowered his voice confidentially. "I try to know all the students, so that whenever they come to my office for breaking the rules, I can talk to them and settle the matter amicably. But I make a mistake sometimes and misjudge one of them," he added.

Mom nodded her head agreeably, Pacified by his apology, she could afford to be civil now. "I understand how that could happen," she said. "I can't dispute the wisdom of the way you run things here. Lord knows, I wouldn't have the patience to handle the young ones the way you do."

Mr. Drayer and Mom smiled at each other, then turned toward me and frowned. Aunt Fanny, sitting quietly beside Mom, was staring at a spot over my head, removing herself from any part of what was going on.

I turned my eyes to meet Mr. Drayer's disapproving gaze.

"Seely," he said. "You know it is against the rules to leave this building during school hours. Yet you have done so time after time with no regard for the rules. Do you think this is right? Fair for you, but not for the others?"

"No, sir."

"Then why did you leave the school yesterday, after I finished talking to you here in the office?"

"I didn't feel good," I said.

"In other words," he said, "you felt bad about what you'd done, and you were sorry you'd done it?"

"No, sir," I replied. "I wasn't sorry I'd hit Jummy Lewis. I didn't feel a bit good about it," I added quickly, "but I wasn't sorry. Not till I realized that what I had done would worry Mom and hurt her."

I wouldn't look at Mom and Aunt Fanny. I kept my eyes on Mr. Drayer's face to catch his reaction to my words. "When you said that you'd have to speak to my mother about me, I panicked and ran out of the school-house. It's not Mom's fault that I act the way I do, and I don't think it's right that you should bother her with it."

"That's my job, Seely," Mr. Drayer said patiently. "When you kids are unruly, it is my practice to call in your parents, talk to them, and see if we can get to the bottom of whatever is troubling you."

I stood before him, my arms straight at my sides, and

194

my head down. I couldn't tell him what was troubling me. Not with Mom sitting there, listening to me.

"When I lost my husband"—Mom spoke quietly, her voice low—"it seemed like there was no way I could go on alone. I shut myself away from the young'uns and Seely had to handle everything by herself. She has chopped the wood, cooked the meals, and seen to it that her brother Robert had clean clothes to wear to school. I've been no help to her at all. More of a care than anything else," she added.

I raised my eyes. Mr. Drayer was nodding his head thoughtfully. I glanced at Mom, then quickly back to the floor at my feet. Her face was so sad and heavy-hearted that I just ached for her. I knew what it must have cost Mom to bare her soul to someone she hardly knew. And she had done it to excuse my behavior.

"Seely, why didn't you come to me?" Mr. Drayer spoke gently, yet with a trace of impatience that I hadn't called on him for help. "I could've done something for you."

When he called my name, I raised my head and kept my eyes on him. "It was no hardship, Mr. Drayer. There was nothing anyone could do that I wasn't doing already. But, lately, Mom has been like her old self again, and I wanted to keep her that way. That's why I was afraid to have you tell her that I'd hit Jummy Lewis. I couldn't bear to be the cause of her getting sick and all upset again," I added, my voice near to breaking.

He gave Mom a bit of a smile. "I think Seely can stop

195

worrying about your health," he said kindly. "Isn't that right, Mrs. Robinson?"

He didn't wait for an answer from Mom, but turned once more to face me. "We're going to forget that you left school yesterday without permission," Mr. Drayer said. "We'll let it pass as if it had never happened. But one more such instance, or if I hear of you leaving this schoolhouse at any time, you'll answer to both your mother and me for it."

"Seely knows right from wrong," Mom spoke up. "She's not likely to go against the rules deliberately."

She would have gone on, but the principal broke in on her. "Excuse me, Mrs. Robinson." He looked at his watch. "It's time for Seely's next class." Then to me, he said, "You may go now," and motioned toward the door.

I ducked my head and mumbled, "Yes, sir." I gave Mom and Aunt Fanny a quick glance, then I turned and left the room.

I suspected that I had been sent away so they could talk about me without my ears hearing everything they said. Mr. Drayer probably figured he would settle the matter of my nonconformity while he had Mom here at school. But if Mom was feeling as well as she appeared to be, I thought, he would have more of a fight on his hands than he had anticipated. Mom didn't conform to a lot of his beliefs and practices, any more than I did.

I barely had time to get back to my desk when the bell rang for second period English class. I grabbed my book and notebook and hurried to catch up with Roxie and Annabel.

196

"Did you catch hell from your mother and Mr. Drayer?" Roxie whispered. "He was laying down the law to me when your mother stormed into his office, madder than a wet hen. I figured then that you were in for it," she added.

I shook my head no. "They just told me not to leave the schoolhouse again, or I'd really be in trouble."

Annabel giggled, and as we entered the classroom, she said, "I used to hold the record for getting sent to the principal's office, but you two have kept him so busy lately that now he just nods his head and sends me back to class."

Miss Hendricks put her fingers to her lips, frowned, and shook her head at us. We hushed and took our seats. But we didn't learn anything in class that day. I was too concerned with what was going on in the office between Mom and Mr. Drayer, and Roxie and Annabel were curious about what ailed me.

As we were leaving the classroom, I glanced down the hall toward the library and Mr. Drayer's office. The door was wide open, and I couldn't see anyone in the room. Mom and Aunt Fanny had gone, and there was no sign of Mr. Drayer anywhere. I went through the rest of the day in a stupor. One minute I was anxious for the day to end, and the next I wished it never would. I dreaded to hear what Mom would have to say to me when I got home.

I just halfway heard Peedle Porter's chatter on the school bus, and I hardly noticed when he and Annabel and the Knight boys got off. I was so deep in thought that Pete Avery had to call my name twice before I heard him.

"Seely, I said a penny for your thoughts," Mr. Avery said.

"You'd be short-changed, Mr. Avery. They're not worth a plugged nickel."

"Then why hold them so close? A body would think you'd found the secret of silence, and you were afraid of breaking it." He chuckled deep inside, as he sought my reflection in his mirror.

I smiled back at Mr. Avery. It was almost impossible not to answer a smile. No matter how worried you might be.

"Mom went to the school today and talked to the principal," I told him. "And heaven only knows—" I stopped, and shook my head. There was no use going on about it. The die had been cast, whatever was decided couldn't be changed by talking and bemoaning the fact. I'd just have to wait and find out for myself.

"Put it out of your mind, Seely," Mr. Avery said. "Your ma is not going to hurt you. She's on your side."

It seemed like the more I worried about something, the less came of it. That afternoon when I got home from school, Mom had plenty to say. But it had nothing to do with me or what had taken place in the principal's office earlier in the day. She had found herself a job and couldn't wait to tell me about it.

Mom said that Fanny Phillips had taken her to every restaurant in Oolitic, and when they were told that these places had no use for homemade pies and cakes, Fanny had driven on to Bedford, to the Graystone Hotel.

"By that time, I was ready to give up and forget the whole idea of selling baked goods," Mom went on. "But fortunately for me, Fanny wouldn't hear of quitting yet. We went inside the hotel and talked to the manager. Then he showed us the way to the kitchen. An hour later when we left the Graystone Hotel, I had the cook's word that he would take a dozen pies this Friday, and a dozen more the first of the week," she added proudly, all out of breath with the telling.

I just stood and looked at her. My heart was so full of pride that I couldn't speak.

There was a bemused look about Mom as she slipped a bib apron over her head and tied the strings. "I know it means a lot of extra work for you, Seely," she said, turning toward the stove to start supper. "It will be up to you to tend the garden, take care of Robert, and see that there's plenty of stove wood on hand. Some days that oven will be going from sun up to sundown, if I'm to make a go of it," she added. "I only wish the confounded thing could hold more than two pies at a time."

"You'll make it all right," I said. "I'll keep the woodbox filled, and Robert won't be any bother. He wants to work in the garden. I'll teach him what to do, and he can help me tend to it. We'll manage just fine," I assured her. "As long as you're here with us."

Mom kind of smiled to let me know she understood what I was trying to say. "I'll have no time to sit twiddling my thumbs this summer," she said. "Not if I aim to get this family back on its feet and off the relief rolls. And besides that," she added, "it's time I took a hand in running things around here. You're getting to be too big for your britches."

She smacked me lightly on the bottom, then gave me a gentle push toward the door. "Get your chores done, Seely," she told me. "We can talk later, after the work's all done."

Robert seemed to grow taller by inches when I told him that he would have charge of the garden. I'd keep an eye on it, see that he was doing things the way he should, but the garden would be his responsibility, I said. We were in the wood yard. I was chopping the wood, and Robert was carrying it to the house. He hadn't touched the axe since I'd bawled him out for trying to use it, and he didn't offer to cut the wood now.

"I could drag some dead wood and fallen limbs from the woods," Robert said. "We'll need it when Mom starts baking all those pies." He gave me a funny look, his head to one side, and asked, "Seely, do you suppose she'll get so tired of making pies that she won't want to make one just for us?"

I set the axe into the chopping block. "We'll have pie," I told Robert. "Someone will have to eat the mistakes she makes."

He giggled, then stooped to gather up the sticks of wood that I had left for him, and we went to the house for supper.

chapter twenty

By Friday morning every flat surface in the kitchen was covered with pies. Mom looked anxiously at them as she waited for Aunt Fanny. "What if folks don't like my pies?" she murmured uneasily.

"They will like them fine," I said. "Why shouldn't they?"

"Oh, I don't know," she answered, leaving the pies to look out the window for Fanny Phillips.

I disliked leaving her alone with her uncertainties, but I had to catch the bus for school. Robert had been gone for quite a while already, and Mr. Avery would be waiting for me. Before I reached the rise in the road, I met Aunt Fanny on her way to our house. I was glad to know that Mom wouldn't have to be alone too long with her doubts and anxiety. Aunt Fanny would reassure her.

For the first time all year, I had to wait for the school bus. And when it finally came in sight, it was coming up the hill, not downhill from Jubilee, the way it usually came. The school bus stopped, and Mr. Avery opened the door.

"Come on, Seely," he said, motioning with his hand. "Ride to the turnaround with me."

I hurried to get on board and slid into the seat directly behind the driver. "Are you late, Mr. Avery? Or am I too early?"

After stopping in the middle of the hill, Mr. Avery was having trouble getting the bus going again. He didn't answer me until we were over the hill, starting down the other side. Then it was more of an explanation than an answer.

"I've been up the better part of the night," he said, his eyes meeting my gaze in the rearview mirror. "Because of the interest I've taken in Morton Chally this past winter, I was called to hear and bear witness to his death-bed confession."

"Chally is dead?" I couldn't believe it.

"And took his time about dying too," Mr. Avery replied, wearily rubbing his hand over his face. "I sat at his bedside from two o'clock this morning till after six, along with three others, writing down every word he uttered."

He paused while he maneuvered the big bus in and out of the wide place in front of Abner Griffin's general store. When we were headed back the way we'd come, Mr. Avery picked up his story where he'd left off.

"I've heard of wicked, evil doings in my time, Seely," he went on, "but I'd swear that Morton Chally topped them all. You can believe me when I say, if he hadn't died, sooner or later someone would've killed him."

I leaned forward in the seat, my head nearly resting on Mr. Avery's shoulder. "Did Chally own up to shooting Russell Williams on purpose?" I asked him. "Or tell why he hated Russell so?"

Mr. Avery nodded his head. "Yes, to both of your questions, Seely. And it wasn't hate as much as it was greed that spurred Chally on to killing."

I sat back in my seat. Now that the truth about how he had died was out in the open, I felt like Russell would rest easier. And that's what I told Pete Avery.

He turned his head to smile at me, then back to the road. "You could be right," Mr. Avery said. "Now that we know the truth, you and I can let him rest."

Nothing else was said until we were passing the abandoned Williams place. Mr. Avery waved his hand toward the burned-out house, the barn, and outbuildings. "Seely, that's what Morton Chally killed three people to get his hands on," he said. "Seems like a mighty dear price to pay for a piece of ground."

"Three people, Mr. Avery? I figured it was only Russell and Lester Graves that he had to answer for."

"Onalee's husband was the first to be got rid of," Mr. Avery said. "Chally killed him, then he threw his body into the pen with that bull. By the time Williams was found there was no way of telling that the bull hadn't killed him.

A chill shook me and raised goose bumps up and down my arms. "Mr. Avery, what makes men do such things?"

He shook his head, as if stumped by my question. "There's no telling, Seely. It began with Cain and Abel, and it won't stop with Morton Chally. There'll always be someone who has something that another will risk killing to get for his own."

Porter Hollow was just around the bend in the road, so by mutual consent neither of us said any more about Morton Chally.

Peedle Porter stopped on the second step up to the bus door and said, "Hey, you're late. What kept you?"

Mr. Avery said, "We're going to be a dang sight later if you don't get on the bus and sit down. Were all the kids like you, Peedle, I'd never get this bus to school on time."

Peedle sat down beside me, and Annabel and Roy Knight sat in the seat behind us. The other Knight boys went to the very last seat in the bus before they sat down. Mr. Avery grumbled loud enough for all to hear, saying he'd sure be glad when this school year was over. He'd had just about all he could stand of kids at this time. He looked in the rearview mirror to make sure the Knight boys were seated before he moved on, and when he caught me watching him, he winked at me and wiped his mouth as if he had just rid himself of a chaw of tobacco.

I guess Peedle Porter must have thought that Mr. Avery's grumbling had been aimed at him. He sat back in his seat and he didn't open his mouth all the way to school. And he was just as quiet on the way home that afternoon.

Mom and Fanny Phillips had heard from Pearl Fiscus, who worked at the Bedford Clinic, that Morton Chally had died of the hog bites, but Pearl had no other details about it. Not that Mom and Fanny cared a whit one way or the other. They were more interested in the seven dollars Mom had been paid for her pies, than the death of that scalawag, as Aunt Fanny called Chally.

They were talking about the money Mom would have on hand by the coming Friday. "Another twelve pies on Monday, and twelve on Friday—why, Zel, that's twenty-one dollars," Aunt Fanny said. "That's better wages than most men are making nowadays."

Mom took a dollar bill from her pocketbook and pressed it into Aunt Fanny's hand. "That's for carrying my baked goods to town for me," she said.

Aunt Fanny put the bill on the table. She wasn't going to take it. Not a penny, she said. But Mom said, "Fanny, if you won't take some pay for hauling me back and forth, then I can't allow you to do it."

Almost quicker than the eye could follow, Aunt Fanny had the money tucked down the front of her dress. "Zel, it looks like you and me are in business." She laughed.

Aunt Fanny left soon afterwards, and Mom went to her bedroom to get out of her good dress and put the money in a safe place. I started to put on a pot of coffee for Mom, but the water bucket was empty. I picked it up and went to the pump on the back porch for water.

Dad used to say if the house caught on fire, the water bucket would be the first thing to burn. I was beginning to believe that. The water bucket was always empty.

While I was priming the pump and catching water for the next priming, Robert came into the backyard dragging a twenty foot long behind him. His face was sweaty and streaked with dirt, and when he dropped the log in the wood yard, he wiped his face with his hands and smeared more grime into the sweat.

I said, "Good heavens, Robert. You didn't have to bring all the woods dirt home with you."

"I've been working," he said, as if the dirt on his face was the proof of his labor.

He came to the pump and rinsed off the biggest share of the black earth and sweat, while I brought him a towel from the kitchen.

"I stopped at Nellie's on the way home from school," Robert said, as he dried himself. "The preacher told me that when the garden stuff came on, what we couldn't use, he'd take on his huckster route and sell it for me."

He ran his fingers through his hair, darker now that it was damp, smoothing it back from his face, and sat down on the porch steps. I sat down beside him.

"What did you tell Mr. Paully about the vegetables?"

Robert turned sober blue eyes on me. "I told him that I 'spected we'd have garden enough to feed half of Greene County, once it got going," He replied seriously, trying his best to be grown-up. "I promised Mr. Paully that I'd gather the stuff, wash it, and get it ready for him to sell. Then he could keep a part of whatever money he got for selling the stuff."

"There's a lot of work to be done in that garden," I said. "And it will be a long time before the vegetables are ready to use."

"That's all right," Robert said. "Our deal will still be good. The preacher and me shook hands on it."

We sat for a while not talking, just putting off the time when we'd have to start on our evening chores. Finally, I said, "Robert, have you told Mom about your agreement with Mr. Paully?"

He shook his head. "I thought I'd wait till I had something to show for it," he said quietly. "Then I'll tell her."

"Then I won't say anything, either," I promised.

Mom and Fanny Phillips made two more trips to Bedford that next week, taking pies to the Graystone Hotel. On their last trip to the hotel, the cook told Mom that they would need three dozen pies a week from now on. Saturday morning Aunt Fanny came to our house to take Mom to do her trading in Oolitic.

Mom had made her grocery list on Friday night after supper, figuring the cost of each item, and adding the column after each one. "We'll have fresh meat and cheese on the table this week," she said, pleased that she could afford such luxuries. She seemed surprised to find that she would have more than half of her money left over when her shopping was all done.

When we'd gotten out of bed on Saturday morning,

207

the sky had been cloudy and overcast, looking to rain any minute. But as we waited for Aunt Fanny to get there, the clouds began to break up and pass over the hills. The sun came out, then went away as a cloud moved across it.

Robert was wishing for rain. He said that the garden was dry as a bone. Mom agreed that the garden could use a good rain, but added that she hoped it would hold off until Fanny Phillips got her car in and out of the dirt lane.

"What do you want Robert and me to do today, while you're gone?" I asked. "There's beds to be changed and a washing to do. And we ought to bring more logs in from the woods. We're getting low on firewood."

"This is no fit day to do a washing," Mom said. "It's likely to rain off and on all day. And we can get the stove wood after we get home from town."

"You mean that Robert and me are going to Oolitic with you?"

This was what I had been wishing for, but with all the work to be done here at home, I didn't think I had one chance in a million of getting to go. Mrs. Avery had sent word by Annabel that she wanted to see me before school was out, but since I'd been forbidden to leave the schoolhouse, there was no way I could go to the Averys' store during the week. Now, I would be able to go see her.

Mom was smiling and nodding her head. "I didn't figure you'd think it such a treat," she said, "seeing as how you have to go to school there every day of the week."

Aunt Fanny said practically the same thing when I

ran out to get in her car. "Lands sakes, Seely, don't you see enough of Oolitic during the school week? I'd think you'd be sick of the place," she said, smiling.

"But this is different," I told her. "I haven't been to town on Saturday since Byron and Johnny Meaders and me used to go have ice cream sodas and window shop, while Mom and Linzy did their trading at the Rainbow Store." I took a breath. "I will sure be glad when Byron gets home. Seems like he's been gone forever."

All at once every one in the car got real quiet. Twenty minutes after the hour, or twenty till, I thought to myself. That's what Dad used to tell us whenever we kids were all quiet at the same time. Aunt Fanny broke the silence.

"Byron won't be coming home this summer," she said. "He wrote his dad that he would be working at learning to run a business, as soon as school was out. That fits right in with his classes at school, and I'm glad he has this chance. But law, how I'm going to miss having that boy around the house."

Mom must have sensed my disappointment. She seemed to know that Fanny's words had taken a big bite out of the pleasure I felt to be going to town today. She turned in her seat to look at me, while she spoke.

"You and Robert can have sodas at the drugstore today," she said gently. "And window wish to your heart's content. Just see that you don't get lost and make Fanny and me come looking for you." Then as an afterthought, she added, "And don't keep us waiting when we're ready to leave for home."

209

As soon as Aunt Fanny stopped the car in the parking lot behind the Rainbow Store, Mom handed us fifty cents and Robert and I headed down the street toward the drug store and a tall, foamy ice cream soda.

"The last time I was here," Robert said, as we crossed the room to a table near the window, "Johnny Meaders had to lift me to the chair. Now I stand tall enough to help myself."

I smiled at him and watched as he seated himself at the same table we had occupied with Johnny and Byron two years ago. Then I took the chair beside Robert and looked out the window.

Big drops of rain spattered the glass. Then it poured for a few minutes, blurring our sight of the sidewalk shoppers as they scrambled for shelter. Robert and I smiled at each other as we watched them, silently congratulating ourselves that we had gotten inside in time and hadn't been caught in the rain.

When our sodas were set in front of us, Robert said, "I'm going to sip this real slow so it will last longer."

"You can't sip too slow," I told him. "When we are finished here, we're going to the south end of town to the Averys' general store."

He took a deep drag on the soda straw, swallowed, and stubborn lines formed around his mouth. I thought he was going to give me an argument about it, but his face cleared and he nodded his head agreeably.

The rain had stopped when we left the drugstore, but the sidewalk was still wet, and water dripped from the buildings. The sun had come out for the moment, but I told Robert it wouldn't last. There were too many clouds in the sky.

"April showers," Robert said, looking knowingly at the sky. "We'll be lucky not to get our butts wet." Then after a few steps he asked, "Seely, why do we have to go to the Averys?"

"Mrs. Avery sent word that she wanted to talk to me," I answered. "I don't know why. But she's been kind to me this past winter, Robert, and I feel obligated to go see her."

It was farther to the Averys' store than I'd thought it would be. We left the town behind us and followed a street where the houses seemed perched on the very edge of the steep ravine that fell away to a valley far below them. I was beginning to think that I had gotten us lost, when I saw the schoolhouse off to the right, at the foot of a hill.

I pointed it out to Robert. "That's where I go to school," I said. "And the Averys' store is just over there."

Robert had been unnaturally quiet for some time. Now, he grinned and gave an exaggerated sigh of relief. "There for a while, Seely, I thought you'd got us lost again."

I didn't see Mrs. Avery anywhere. Pete Avery was working in the store today. He had just finished filling an order for a customer when we walked in, and now he was writing all the articles down in a little book. After he totaled the bill, he tore out the carbon copy and handed it to the waiting customer.

Robert and I were standing near the front of the store,

but I heard the man say, "I'll settle my bill next payday, for sure." And Pete Avery answered, "That's all right, Jeff. Whenever you can spare it." He put the well-used book back under the counter. I wondered if there was a book under the counter with Dad's name on it. And if that was what Mrs. Avery wanted to talk to me about. After all, I was the first one to ever buy something for us on credit from the Averys' store, and I could be held accountable for it, I thought.

When the customer had gone, I took Robert by the hand to go and speak to Mr. Avery. But Robert pulled away and walked to the counter by himself. Mr. Avery seemed pleased to see me, and when I introduced Robert to him, he smiled and shook Robert's hand.

"Mrs. Avery is in the house." He motioned toward a door at the rear of the store. "Go on back and talk to her," he said, "while your brother and me get acquainted."

I left Robert with Mr. Avery and went through the door he had indicated and walked into Mrs. Avery's kitchen. She was busy at the stove, but when she saw me, she pushed the kettle to the back of the stove and came to meet me.

"Seely, I'm glad you could come," she greeted me. "I've been wanting to talk to you about something."

"Annabel told me," I said. "I'd have come to see you before now, but I'm not allowed to leave the schoolhouse since Roxie and I skipped school that day." I took a breath. "Mom came to town today with Fanny Phil-

212

lips to do her trading, so while they're doing that, I came here to see you."

"Then you have no time to waste," Mrs. Avery said. "I'll get right to the point. Seely, we would like to have you come to work for us this summer. Clerking in the store when we need you and helping me here in the house, canning and preserving fruit and cleaning up afterwards."

This was so unexpected, I couldn't say a word. Getting a job and working away from home had never crossed my mind. When I didn't say anything, she smiled at me, then she went on about the job.

"The pay wouldn't be much. Five dollars a week, and your room and board. But we could let you have whatever you want from the store for just what it cost us."

This was the chance of a lifetime, I thought. But I would have to turn it down. There was no way I could take this offer of a job. Not now. Mom couldn't tend the garden, cut wood for the cook stove, and bake thirty-six pies every week, without my help.

"Well, Seely. What do you say? Do you think you'd like living here and working for Mr. Avery and me?"

"Oh, Mrs. Avery, I'd be proud and happy to live here and work for you and Mr. Avery. But I can't this summer. Mom's trying to get back on her feet, working to make a living for us," I explained. "And we've put out this big garden. She couldn't handle everything by herself."

"I understand, Seely." She smiled at me. "I can see

213

your mother needs you more than I do this summer, but maybe by next year . . ."

I answered her smile. "I'll keep that in mind," I said. And went to get Robert. If we hurried, we might get back to the car before Mom came looking for us.

It started to sprinkle as we crossed the street about a block from the parking lot, but it didn't begin to rain in earnest until we were in the car, heading toward home. After asking us if we had liked our sodas, Mom didn't question what we'd done the rest of the time. And I didn't volunteer to tell her.

"We had money coming back when we paid for the sodas," Robert told her.

Mom turned her head to look at him. "Keep it," she said evenly. "It's the last you'll get for foolishness for a while."

She faced forward again, and we were quiet. I think everyone was watching the windshield wipers flapping back and forth, as they cleared a spot for Aunt Fanny so she could see to drive.

The rain had slacked to a slow drizzle by the time we got to our lane, but the chuckholes were full of water, and little rivulets ran down the tracks. Aunt Fanny stopped the car in the middle of the gravel road and turned to Mom with an apologetic smile. "Zel, I hate to leave you here in the rain. But there's no way this old car could make it up that mud road. You know we'd be mired down before we got started."

Mom smiled at Fanny and touched her hand where it held the steering wheel. "You're a good friend, Fanny

Phillips," Mom said. "And I appreciate everything you've done for me. But I won't hear of you apologizing and feeling bad about a little walk in the rain." She kind of laughed. "Fanny, I'm neither sugar nor salt, and I'm nobody's honey. I won't melt."

Mom got out of the car, handed a grocery bag to Robert, and one to me, taking the third and largest sack for herself as she waved Aunt Fanny on her way.

We started up the rain-slick road, the mud clinging to our shoes and gathering more mud with every step. Mom led the way and when she stopped beside the road to clear the mud from her feet on the wet weeds, Robert and I would give our shoes a swipe down each side also.

After one such stop, Mom said. "This reminds me of the day we moved into the Gus Tyson house. Remember, Seely? Even the mule got bogged down in the mud that day." She shifted the heavy grocery sack to the other arm, supporting it with her hand. As we moved on up the hill, Mom went on with her recollections. "I never wanted to live back here in the hills. It was just a place to shelter in. But seemed like once we were settled here, we stayed."

Mom finished with a shake of her head and a deep sigh, and nothing more was said. We concentrated all our effort on keeping our footing on the slick road and our feet free of the dragging mud. We didn't stop to rest again until we reached the top of the hill and saw the house waiting for us about halfway down the other side.

"With the help of you two kids," Mom said, when she had caught her breath, "I figure we can be away from

215

here by fall. We've no kin, nor close ties, just Nellie and Aunt Fanny, to hold us here, and you'll both be better off away from these hills and hollows."

Robert's eyes got wide and a little frightened at the thought of making a change, but he didn't say anything. Neither did I. I held my breath and waited to hear what else Mom had to say. It was plain from the way she held herself that she had made up her mind about this, and she was determined to go through with it.

"I've done a lot of thinking these past weeks," Mom said. "At first I put my hopes in the garden, selling everything we could grow and using the money to get off the welfare rolls. Then when Fanny came up with the idea of selling baked goods and the hotel bought them, I knew that would be the way." She paused and wiped the mist of rain from her face. "I'm going to save every penny I make from baking pies, and by the first of September we'll have enough money to move to Bedford, close to my work and to good schools for you two young'uns. We'll be off relief, and welfare will be a thing of the past."

Mom took a tighter grip on the dampened sack and started on down the hill.

"But we don't know anyone in Bedford," I said. "What if we needed something? Who could we go to there?"

Mom turned to look at me, then kept right on going down the road. "We're going to learn to depend on ourselves," she said fiercely. "As for friends, we'll make new ones. We didn't know anyone when we came here," she reminded me. When she next spoke, her voice was low, almost gentle. "Seely, we have come to the end of this dark road. We can go no farther. But at every end there's a new beginning. And that's what we've got to look forward to."

I counted that rainy afternoon as our new beginning. From that time on we worked for just one purpose, getting off welfare and getting out of Greene County, which Mom classed as one and the same. Robert and I tended the garden, then scoured the woods for dead logs that we could drag home and cut up for firewood. Mom baked pies in the heat of the day, the old wood-burning cookstove adding another hundred degrees to the heat outside.

School ended for the year, and as each one waved goodbye and called, "See you next year," I just lifted my hand and didn't answer.

The Reverend Mr. Paully held prayer meeting in the schoolhouse in Jubilee on Sunday night, then came by our place every Monday morning with his huckster wagon to collect the garden stuff that Robert had ready for him. With the exception of what we ate at our table, Robert sold every vegetable that grew in our garden. And he handed the money to Mom to add to our savings.

I didn't even notice when the cardboard relief boxes stopped coming to our house. I only know that when Mom started packing our stuff to move from Gus Tyson's house, she couldn't find a single box to put anything in.

217